Think of Me

Also by Jane McBride Choate in Large Print:

Badge of Love
The Courtship of Katie McGuire
Love and Lies
Love by the Book
A Match Made in Heaven
Mustang Summer
Trust Me
Design to Deceive
Sweet Lies and Rainbow Skies

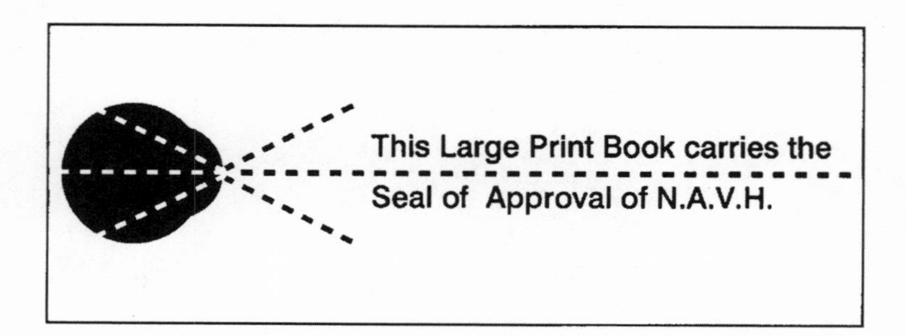

Think of Me

Jane McBride Choate

Thorndike Press • Waterville, Maine

Published in 2004 by arrangement with Jane McBride Choate.

Thorndike Press® Large Print Candlelight.

The tree indicium is a trademark of Thorndike Press.

The text of this Large Print edition is unabridged.
Other aspects of the book may vary from the original edition.

Set in 16 pt. Plantin by Elena Picard.

Printed in the United States on permanent paper.

Library of Congress Cataloging-in-Publication Data

Choate, Jane McBride.
Think of me / Jane McBride Choate.
p. cm.
ISBN 0-7862-7047-0 (lg. print : hc : alk. paper)
1. Women weavers — Fiction. 2. Legislators — Fiction.
3. Large type books. I. Title.
PS3553.H575T47 2004
813′.54—dc22 2004056742

For Rita Cochrane Droter,
precious friend and "adopted sister"

National Association for Visually Handicapped
serving the partially seeing

As the Founder/CEO of NAVH, the only national health agency solely devoted to those who, although not totally blind, have an eye disease which could lead to serious visual impairment, I am pleased to recognize Thorndike Press* as one of the leading publishers in the large print field.

Founded in 1954 in San Francisco to prepare large print textbooks for partially seeing children, NAVH became the pioneer and standard setting agency in the preparation of large type.

Today, those publishers who meet our standards carry the prestigious "Seal of Approval" indicating high quality large print. We are delighted that Thorndike Press is one of the publishers whose titles meet these standards. We are also pleased to recognize the significant contribution Thorndike Press is making in this important and growing field.

Lorraine H. Marchi, L.H.D.
Founder/CEO
NAVH

* Thorndike Press encompasses the following imprints: Thorndike, Wheeler, Walker and Large Pr int Press.

Prologue

Carla Hastings placed her hand over her rounded middle, an instinctive gesture as the baby stirred within her. Her sigh of relief whispered out at the slight flutter — a definite relief compared to the tightening in her womb that had occurred earlier today.

Without warning, the baby kicked vigorously, a series of sharp raps, as if he were somersaulting. Or jogging. Or warming up for a hockey game. A few minutes later, he settled down.

She shifted to ease the kink in her lower back. Her back had been aching all day. It was little wonder, considering she was carrying around an extra twenty-five pounds. Still, it had never throbbed quite this way before. She shrugged away the discomfort and turned her attention to her notes.

"Carla, are you all right?"

She looked up to find her friend Eve

Dalton watching her with concern. "I'm fine. Sam Junior is just letting me know he's still here." She glanced down at the mound of her eight-months-plus pregnant self.

The morning sickness — all three months of it, the swollen feet, the constant trips to the bathroom, had all been worth it. The knowledge that she was carrying a new life within her, a life she and Sam had created together, was a constant source of wonder for her.

The pain in her back intensified. She rubbed at it, hoping to massage it away. It persisted, though, and she changed positions again.

Jeanette Hastings, Carla's mother-in-law, frowned. "You're pushing yourself too hard. Sam would have my head if he knew I was letting you sit in on today's meeting. You promised him you'd go home and rest before the auction."

Carla made a face, even as her heart picked up its beat at the mention of her husband. Two years married and she still blushed like a new bride whenever she thought of Sam. "Sam treats me like I'm made of china."

"He loves you," Eve said quietly. "Besides, he's about to become a father. The man's entitled to act a little crazy."

The three women laughed. That eased the tension, and Carla threw her friend a grateful look. Eve had been a lifesaver during the last few weeks. The two had met while raising money for scholarships for inner-city children and had become fast friends. Eve shared Carla's commitment to helping kids plus a quirky sense of humor that relieved even the most tense situation.

A weaver who managed and owned a yarn and design shop, Eve had sponsored Ron Franks, a young friend of Carla and Sam's, offering him an afternoon job and, more importantly, faith in him. Carla knew, better than most, what that belief meant to a teenage boy who rubbed uncomfortably against the edges of adulthood.

Another flutter. She ignored it and concentrated on the task at hand. "Come on. We've got an auction to put the final touches on."

An auction to raise funds had been Jeanette's idea. Carla's mother-in-law had proven invaluable in organizing, advertising, and finding a place to hold the event.

Carla winced as a tiny heel — or was it

an elbow — pressed against her belly. She'd grown accustomed to the sensation of a heel or fist or elbow poking her at inconvenient times, but this felt different somehow.

The pain sharpened, quickened until she could no longer ignore it. She changed positions and nearly doubled over. The flutter had grown into a full-fledged contraction.

Jeanette took Carla's hand in her own. "You're having contractions, aren't you?"

Carla nodded and flattened a hand against her stomach, trying to ease the growing pressure there. It was probably just false labor. She wouldn't panic. Hadn't she read somewhere that first babies were rarely early?

The pain had spread, settling in the small of her back. She glanced at her watch and timed the next one. Ten minutes. Too soon to start planning the trip to the hospital. The next one kicked in at a little less than eight. All pretense of working ceased as the three women kept their gazes trained on the clock.

First babies aren't supposed to be early, she reminded herself, and then wondered if Sam Junior had read the same book she had.

By the time the contractions reached a six-minute interval, she was panting. "I think . . . I think we'd better get to the hospital."

Jeanette took charge with scarcely a ripple. "Eve, help Carla to the car. I'll call Sam."

Sam Hastings looked at the choked downtown Saratoga traffic in front of him, then at his watch, then at the taxi driver — all for the tenth time in as many seconds.

Of all days for his car to be in the shop. The call from his mother had him racing from a city council meeting and hailing a taxi.

"Can't you find a way around this mess?" he asked, knowing there was none.

The harried driver shot Sam an annoyed look over his shoulder. "Look, mister, if you're in such a hurry, why don't you get out and walk?"

"Good idea." Sam threw a couple of bills onto the front seat and pushed open the door.

"Hey, I was just kidding," the driver yelled.

"I wasn't."

"What's so important?"

"My wife's having a baby." Sam slammed

the door behind him and took off running, his prayers keeping pace with his feet as they slapped the pavement. Grateful for the early morning runs Carla had addicted him to, he kept up a steady stride. Joggers weren't uncommon in Saratoga's parks. But a man in a three-piece business suit cutting through the streets at midday was enough to attract more than a few stares.

He ignored them.

All that mattered was that he reach the hospital on time. Why hadn't he stayed home today? He'd even suggested it, but Carla had insisted he go on to work. She'd steadfastly refused his efforts to pamper her during the last months.

He sprinted through the hospital doors. Deciding the elevators were too slow, he took the stairs two at a time. "Carla Hastings." He managed to pant out the words at the nurses' station on the fourth floor.

The nurse looked him over. "Funny. You don't look like a Carla." His scowl silenced her. "Sorry. It's been a long day." She checked a chart. "Mrs. Hastings is in room 412."

Eve and Jeanette alternated between pacing and downing cups of coffee. When

Gerald Hastings joined them, Eve excused herself, leaving the two grandparents-to-be alone. She kept an eye on her watch, figuring she had an hour and forty-five minutes, two hours at the most, before she had to leave to dress for the auction.

She wasn't officially in charge, but she'd promised Carla she'd be there to oversee it. Thank goodness they already had an auctioneer.

When Sam emerged from the delivery room an hour later, he had tears in his eyes. "It's a boy."

Eve waited with the senior Hastings to see Zachary Samuel Hastings at the nursery window. "There he is," she pointed as a nurse held up a baby with a tuft of dark hair peeking from the white knit hat covering his head.

Gerald Hastings clapped his son on his back, tears glistening against his ruddy cheeks. Jeanette cried openly as she hugged Sam.

Eve knew enough of the history of the family, the estrangement between Sam and his parents that had only recently been bridged, to understand the miracle she was witnessing.

Chapter One

Normally Eve Dalton avoided fund-raisers. She left them to the movers and shakers of the city who chased after power and prestige. The cheek-bussing and hand-pumping were nothing more than a polite camouflage for society's version of robbery. That tonight's version was organized by a friend's mother wasn't enough to induce her to attend, much less help.

No, she was here because she believed in the cause. She gave her passion and her energy wherever her heart dictated. So far, it hadn't led her wrong.

She pulled on a velvet skirt and topped it with a crocheted vest of cobweb-fine yarn, leaving her arms bare. The effect was feminine, soft, and a touch eccentric. She wound her hair in a French braid and settled for a quick dab of lipstick as her only makeup.

Carla wasn't able to be there, but Eve

was determined to make the night a success. Jeanette Hastings had put together a dynamite collection of services to be auctioned off. A smile slipped across Eve's lips as she thought of Jeanette's original idea — a bachelor auction.

Carla had tactfully nixed that with a suggestion of a service auction. Jeanette had seized upon that with a zeal that Eve could only envy, extracting promises from dozens of people to contribute. The services she'd secured ranged from furniture refinishing to dog grooming, art restoration to plumbing, a diaper service to a ride in a hot-air balloon.

In addition, Jeanette, in the most ladylike manner possible, had strong-armed the use of a mansion from one of her society friends to hold tonight's auction.

The auction had started off with bidding for a meal for eight catered by a chef of a five-star hotel. It netted several thousand dollars.

Daniel Cameron was accustomed to fund-raisers. That tonight's affair was for charity rather than for political reasons didn't change the nature of it. Men and women dressed to impress, jewels removed from safes to adorn and embellish, smiles ready in case the camera flashed their way. He didn't mind the trappings; they were part and parcel of the package, a slick and glossy package.

He wasn't here as a political figure but as a friend. Sam Hastings was one of the few people Daniel knew who wasn't impressed by Daniel Cameron, United States senator. College roommates more years ago than he cared to count, they had kept in touch despite the different paths their lives had taken.

Sam had called shortly before the auction was due to begin to tell Daniel about the baby.

"That's great, buddy. Congratulations." Daniel listened some more. "Yeah. When can I see Carla and the baby? Tomorrow night? Right."

"You're not off the hook on going to the auction, buddy," Sam had said. "I expect you to drop a bundle tonight. It's for a good cause."

After promising to bid on something, Daniel had congratulated his friend again and hung up.

One of Saratoga's older homes, a Georgian-style mansion, was the setting for the auction. When he arrived, the bidding was already under way on flying lessons from a local aviation school.

Good-natured competition carried the bid up to five hundred dollars for three lessons.

Daniel watched as one item after another was sold. He calculated the evening's take thus far to be a little over twenty thousand dollars. After bidding on and winning a day at a health spa, which he intended to give to his mother, he felt free to indulge in his hobby of people-watching.

A husky laugh had snared his attention, and he turned in that direction. The woman it belonged to was a surprise. In a room where most of the women were clones of each other, she stood out. Her skirt and vest weren't from a shop catering to society wives. They were as vivid and unusual as the woman herself.

She didn't bid on the items most women were interested in — the appointment with a prestigious salon, the dress worn by a '30s Hollywood star, or the glamour shots by a famous photographer. No, a diaper service had caught her interest. She wasn't a flashy bidder, but a relentless one. Her bids rose by small but steady amounts until the service was hers.

Hair too bright to be called auburn and too dark to be titian rained down her back in an intricately coiled braid. But it wasn't that which held his interest. A face too animated to be truly beautiful nevertheless compelled the viewer to take a second look. But that wasn't the draw for him either. Her laugh invited others to join in. Even that wasn't what attracted him.

It was something in the eyes, he decided. A vibrancy, a touch of mischief, a fresh way of looking at the world, perhaps. She was a woman who drew a man's gaze, not because she was beautiful, although she was far from plain, but because she compelled attention.

She was, Daniel decided, not a woman to be ignored.

He watched as she tried to make her way to where the food waited, pausing to talk with a group here, another there. Others sought her out. Her easy way with people wasn't affected. He'd seen enough of its counterfeit to recognize the genuine article. She listened to everyone with the same sincere interest.

He knew colleagues who paid handsomely to have others advise them on how to achieve that same ease with people. What they didn't realize was that the real thing couldn't be bought.

Reality brought him up short. A diaper

service meant babies. And babies most likely meant she was married. The disappointment he felt was way out of line. He'd seen her only from a distance, had never talked with her, and yet he was drawn to her in a way he couldn't explain.

When she retired with her prize, he lost interest in the bidding and decided to visit the buffet table.

The organizers had spared no expense, providing an impressive array of food. After choosing jumbo shrimp and lobster pastries, he leaned against a marble column and prepared to enjoy himself.

Eve had felt the dark-haired man's gaze on her for the last few minutes. He was six-feet-plus of pure male.

It was the artist in her, she decided, that gave her a healthy sense of appreciation for sheer male beauty. Easily the best-looking man in the room, he looked like a young Robert Redford with a little Kevin Costner thrown in.

He looked spectacular in his tux, but then, she imagined, he'd look just as good in casual clothes. It was more than a physical attraction, though. It was something about the way he carried himself, a self-assurance that said he knew who he was and was comfortable with it.

Their gazes caught, connected. Her skin prickled with tension as he made no pretense of pretending not to stare at her. The room receded around them, and, for a moment, it was just the two of them. Muted voices, like lapping waves, ebbed and swelled around them, no more than background noise to the rapid tattoo of her heart. Awareness arched between them, an intangible but nonetheless real force. A rush of air signaled that she'd been holding her breath. She inhaled sharply, hoping the influx of oxygen would clear her head.

It didn't work.

Tension shimmered in waves so intense that she was surprised the air didn't snap and crackle with electricity. She shifted her gaze, and the spell was broken.

She started toward the buffet table again, only to be waylaid by a husband and wife who'd just purchased a grooming service for their twin poodles and were eager to share their good fortune.

She made the appropriate remarks and made her escape. Her stomach voiced its displeasure at having missed both lunch and dinner. Intent on reaching the smorgasbord, she ran into a hard wall. Strong hands steadied her. She looked up into a pair of pewter-gray eyes. *His.*

"I'm sorry," she said, trying to sidestep.

"I'm not." He dropped his hands, but their warmth on the bare skin of her arms remained.

His smile was so engaging that she felt her own lips curve in response.

"I'm trying to make it to the buffet table and keep getting sidetracked."

"I saw. How about if I run interference for you?" He cupped her elbow and steered her toward the food-laden table. With him as her escort, she found the path suddenly clear.

"Try the shrimp," he said. "They're delicious."

She bit into a particularly succulent jumbo shrimp. "Mmm." She polished off two more shrimp and a couple of crab cakes before she tried to make conversation. "I missed dinner," she confided.

"I would never have known," he said, straight-faced.

Unoffended, she proceeded to fill her plate. She'd spent two hours seeing to the behind-the-scenes workings of the auction and then making small talk. Now she needed sustenance. After working her way down the table, she headed back to where she'd left him standing.

His lips quirked as he took in the

amount of food on her plate. "I like a woman who knows how to enjoy food."

"Then you ought to love me," she said without thinking. She didn't need to touch her cheeks to know they were hot with color.

"You could be right," he said, his eyes on her hand.

That wasn't what she'd expected to hear.

"You bought a diaper service," he commented.

Had he been watching her during the bidding? Well, she couldn't complain. Not when she'd been doing the same thing. "It's a present. For a friend." At his intent look, she explained. "She just had a baby. Today."

"You aren't married." The words held more than casual interest.

"No." Uncomfortable with his scrutiny, she popped a triangle of caviar-topped toast into her mouth, then picked another one for him. "Here."

"Thanks."

"It's the least I could do since you saved me from a slow and painful death." At his raised brows, she explained. "Starvation."

"My pleasure."

She liked him. Maybe it was the way he entered into her nonsense without a qualm. Maybe it was his serious eyes that still managed to glint with humor.

She'd always believed in going with her instincts and held out her hand. "Eve Dalton. I think I'm going to like you."

Her candid statement brought a smile to his lips as his hand folded around hers. "Daniel. Do you always say what you think?"

Gently, she tugged her hand free. "Almost always." Was it her imagination, or did his hand linger before sliding away from hers?

"Only almost?"

"I don't believe in absolutes."

"What do you believe in?"

"People." Without apology, she changed the subject. "It went well tonight."

"I've had my pockets picked in Washington and didn't lose as much as I did tonight."

She wrestled with a smile. And lost. "Think of the bright side: this goes to help send needy kids to college."

"You like kids?"

"Yes. I do."

"So do I." An answering smile touched his mouth. "I have a feeling we have a lot in common."

"Such as?"

"Do you like lobster?"
"Who doesn't?"
"Chocolate?"
"The richer, the better."
"Pizza?"
"Of course."
"There." The word held a wealth of satisfaction. "We have more in common than you thought."
His grin was so smug that she couldn't keep back the laugh that bubbled out. "Kids, lobster, and chocolate don't make a relationship."
"Don't forget the pizza."
She rolled her eyes. "Like that makes a difference?"
He looked surprised. "You're questioning the power of pizza?"
"Never. That would be un-American."
"It's settled then. We're soul mates. Have dinner with me tomorrow night."
She flashed him a smile. "Now why would I be wanting to do that when I don't even know your full name?"
He looked surprised, then amused. "Cameron. Daniel Cameron."
"Well, Daniel Cameron, I'd be pleased . . ."
Daniel Cameron. *Of course.* Hometown boy who went to the nation's capital and

made good. If she hadn't been caught up in the mechanics of the auction, she'd have put it together sooner. Her sigh was barely audible, but he must have noticed.

Her withdrawal was almost a tangible thing. She wrapped herself up in her own thoughts and seemed to move away from him, though she didn't take a step.

"I'm sorry, Senator. I don't date politicians." She forced a smile to her lips, tried to make it reflect in her eyes, and knew she hadn't succeeded.

He'd been so busy enjoying their banter and the sweet scent of her hair that he almost didn't hear her. When the meaning of her words penetrated, he gave her a quizzical look. "You're kidding. Right?" The humor in his eyes invited her to agree, to take back her words.

"I'm sorry," she repeated.

The amusement faded, to be replaced by a thoughtful frown. "You're serious, aren't you?"

"Look, Senator. I like you."

Was that regret in her voice? A faint smile skipped across his lips, "That sounds like the beginnings of a brush-off."

"Not a brush-off. That would mean there was something between us. Think of it as 'Thanks, but no thanks.' "

"Let me get this straight. We've known each other less than . . ." he checked his watch ". . . ten minutes and you've already made up your mind about me?"

"If you like."

"I don't." He spread his hands, the gesture at once a plea and a command. "We're not going to fall in love over one dinner." The words lingered in the air, and he wondered if he would remember them for the rest of his life.

Her eyes widened, but she kept her smile in place. "Senator —"

"The name's Daniel."

"Senator," she said firmly. "Let's chalk it up to being the right person with the wrong job."

"Wrong for whom?"

"Me." she said quietly, and started to walk away.

A hand clamped on her arm, holding her still. "So far you've done all the rule-setting. Now it's my turn."

"Okay, Senator," she said with only the slightest emphasis on the word. Color bloomed on her cheeks. He'd annoyed her. Good. That was better than indifference. "Let's have it."

Their faces were scant inches apart, and his breath brushed across her face.

"Number one, I like you. Number two, you like me. That leads us to number three. We get to know each other better."

"Wrong." She held up three fingers, ticking off her points. "Number one, I choose who I want to spend time with. Number two, I've already made my choice. Number three, I don't date senators. Not even the good-looking ones." There it was again. Definitely regret. The first man in more months than she wanted to count who'd sparked any interest and he was off-limits. That those limits were self-imposed didn't alter the seriousness with which she took them.

"Why?"

"Let's just say I'm not into the political scene."

"I'm a man first, a politician second."

"Sorry." She really was. "I can't separate the two."

"Try."

"No." The uncompromising tone of her voice had him raising his brows.

"You sound very sure about this."

"I am."

"Care to tell me why?" he asked.

"You've been in politics long enough to understand policy-making. I have my own policy." He waited. "I don't date senators."

A muscle ticked in his neck, but he gave no other sign that her words bothered him. "Is it just senators, or does your policy include anyone connected with politics?"

"I don't have to explain myself. Not to you, not to anyone."

"Are you always this rude, or is it only my presence that brings it out?"

She flushed. He was right. She had been rude. That didn't mean she was going to change her mind. Not about him. "Excuse me, please."

He fitted a finger beneath her chin, bringing her head up so that her gaze was on a level with his own. "You'll think of me tonight."

She wanted to rail at the arrogance of it, but she couldn't. It wasn't an order, but a statement of fact.

Before he could stop her, she slipped through the crowd. He didn't try following her.

Eve barely noticed as the guests started leaving, air-kissing each other. Normally, she disliked the empty gesture. Tonight she gave scant heed as one person after another performed the ritual against her cheek.

Why did the one man who'd stirred any interest in her in months have to be a politician?

With customary resolve, she forced him from her mind. Chances were she'd never see him again. He obviously traveled in different circles than she did. That they'd met tonight was a fluke. Daniel Cameron was an influential man, one who wielded power with the same style with which he wore evening clothes. He belonged to a world she'd left years ago, one she had no intention of returning to.

She'd seen how politics turned lives inside out. On occasion, it even took them. She wouldn't be a part of that. Not ever again.

Still, she couldn't completely banish the memory of him.

At home, Daniel thought about the woman who'd dismissed him for no better reason than that she didn't like his profession. The unfairness of it offended his sense of justice.

But it was more than that.

He wasn't accustomed to people challenging him. Maybe it came from being the oldest son in a large family. Maybe it came from being a United States senator. Maybe it came from a lot of things. The only thing he knew for sure was that he didn't like it.

There were any number of women who'd be more than happy to spend some time with him. But he'd discovered something along the way. He didn't want any number of women. He surprised himself with the admission. Her openness, her candor, even her disdain of his profession had challenged him.

Anticipation brought a smile to his lips. He had a feeling the lady could become special to him. It might be interesting to find out. He was enough of a strategist to bide his time. There'd be another time. He'd make sure of it.

Chapter Two

She'd slept poorly.

She blamed that on Daniel Cameron. He'd been right. She *had* thought of him. Most of the night had been spent doing exactly that.

Annoyance mixed with amusement. The annoyance was directed at herself; the amusement at him. He'd invaded her dreams, and now thoughts of him were filling her daytime hours as well. She had to hand it to him, she thought with a scowl.

Her lips softened as she thought of the kids who would benefit from last night's auction. Nearly twenty-five thousand dollars was enough to provide tuition for a couple of kids. And with more pledges coming in, the fund would grow. A financial counselor had offered to invest the money.

It was a start.

Eve believed in people. If she had an investment principle, it was to put her resources in people and watch them grow. In return, they rarely disappointed her.

Some might call her naive. She was enough of a pragmatist to recognize the charge held an element of truth. She was enough of a dreamer to ignore it. Given the choice, she'd choose dreamer over pragmatist any day of the week.

Dreams, as fine as the mohair yarn she spun now, kept the world turning. They colored the gray days and added depth to the bright ones. They gave her strength when her own was flagging. They were the only reality she wanted to believe in.

A politician wasn't likely to understand.

Darn it. She was doing it again. Thinking of him. Hadn't he told her she would? She didn't like it. Being predictable was tantamount to being boring. She didn't intend on being either. Not when life beckoned with its infinite variations. Not when she had any say in the matter.

A small voice whispered that she had lost her say last night when Daniel Cameron had closed his hand around hers and pulled her to him. Memories of the way his gaze had connected with hers, the warmth of his fingers pressed against her own, the challenge she'd read in his eyes, skittered over her.

Determinedly, she ignored them.

Dreams. She'd concentrate on dreams. He had no place in her dreams. She conjured up her latest one: a scholarship program established for children who showed artistic promise but had no way to turn that promise into fact.

The proceeds from last night's auction would go a long way toward making that dream a reality.

Dreams and reality. The two could peacefully coexist. Could a dreamer and a politician find the same harmony?

No.

She glanced at the clock. Only two hours to go before hospital visiting hours started. A smile brushed her lips as she thought of Carla and the new baby.

Eve arrived with only minutes to spare before visiting hours began. The hospital smelled of flowers and antiseptic, with a bit of pine cleanser thrown in for good measure. She clutched a yellow pig in one hand and a box of chocolates in the other.

She was about to knock on Carla's door when Daniel Cameron rounded the corner. She knew a flash of pleasure, followed by a quick surge of anger. Was the man following her? She lifted her chin and held her ground.

"You." Her pulse picked up its beat.

His smile widened. "You remember."

She wasn't likely to forget the man who'd occupied her dreams of last night and her thoughts for most of the day, but she hadn't expected to see him again. Certainly not at the hospital visiting Carla Hastings. She'd been trying for hours to keep from thinking about him, keep from picturing him in her mind, telling herself that an attraction to someone so totally wrong for her was crazy.

Nevertheless, his handsome features had popped into her thoughts every other minute, causing a tingling sensation to dance down her spine, the same one that even now threatened to turn her into a gibbering idiot.

"What are you doing here?" The words came before she could stop them. Her flush drew a smile from him. "I'm sorry. I didn't mean —" Darn. Why was she always letting her mouth run away from her around this man?

"I'm a friend of Carla and Sam Hastings," he said.

"So am I."

"Something else we have in common," he murmured.

She ignored that. "I didn't know you

knew Carla and Sam."

"Sam and I were roommates at Stanford. I try to stop in and see him and Carla whenever I'm in town."

"Oh." *Good answer, Dalton.* First she couldn't keep quiet and now all she could come up with was "Oh."

"How about you?" he asked.

"Carla and I were both on the auction committee." There was more, much more, to their friendship than that, but she wasn't about to share it.

"That's who you bought the diaper service for?"

She nodded. "It's great about the baby."

"Yeah. Who's that?" he asked, pointing to the yellow pig.

"Chester."

"Chester, meet Wilbert."

He held up a huge stuffed walrus. Green with huge purple tusks, it had an endearing smile that had her lips edging up in response.

She tried to keep a straight face, but the grin slipped out anyway. "Wilbert?"

"Yeah." Daniel twirled Wilbert's whiskers around his finger. "Doesn't he look like one?"

She tilted her head to one side and pretended to study the ridiculous-looking animal. "I'd say he was more a Herbert."

Daniel made a sound of disgust. "What kind of name is Herbert? No self-respecting walrus would be caught dead with a name like that."

She assumed a fierce expression which failed to stop a smile from twitching at her lips. "I'll have you know my great-grandfather was a Herbert."

"You have a beautiful smile." He didn't touch her, but his voice was a caress in itself.

"We were talking about Herberts."

"Not anymore." He slipped his free arm around her waist.

"Why?" she asked, trying to ignore the warmth of his hand as it settled at the small of her back.

"Why what?"

She remembered he'd made her smile the night before. It felt good then. It felt good now. "Why do I think I'm going to end up liking you anyway?"

His smile was lethal. "You can't help yourself?"

She managed to slide free of his hold and instantly regretted the loss of contact. "I'll just have to try harder." That, more than anything, convinced her she'd be wise to keep her distance.

His smile turned faintly quizzical, but he didn't object. He knocked lightly on the door.

"Come in," Sam's voice called.

Sam Hastings stood by the bed, his hand resting on Carla's shoulder. She looked prettier than ever, Eve thought. A feeling of peaceful serenity had added to Carla's beauty. Flowers filled the room, but they paled in comparison to the light that shone from her eyes.

Eve said as much, causing her friend to blush. "It's Sam and Zach," Carla said softly. "I never knew it was possible to be this happy." She reached for her husband's hand.

Sam looked down at his wife with such tender love in his eyes that it brought tears to Eve's own.

Feeling she was intruding upon a private moment, Eve turned away. Her gaze connected with Daniel's. The understanding she read in his face told her he shared her feelings. He held out his hand. Together, they tiptoed from the room.

In the hallway, she searched through her purse for a tissue and found a linen handkerchief pressed into her hand. "Thanks." She swiped at her eyes. "You're all right, Senator."

"So are you."

"I'm not one of those women who weep at weddings and . . ." The tears started again.

Daniel took the handkerchief from her and dabbed at her eyes. "I can see that."

"I'm not," she insisted, and took it back from him to blow her nose.

Sam came out a few minutes later, a sheepish expression on his face. "Sorry. We tend to forget anyone else is around."

Daniel clapped him on the back. "You're entitled, buddy."

"Yeah," Sam said with new-father pride. "I guess I am at that." He cleared his throat. "Come back in."

Eve and Daniel took turns kissing Carla and handed her the gifts.

She oohed and aahed over them, setting the stuffed animals next to the bed. The box of chocolates she kept by her side.

"They're trying to starve me in here," she confided. "I'm going to need these." She opened the box and popped a candy in her mouth. "Mmmm." She passed around the box. The others declined, earning a smile from her.

"Take Daniel up to see Zachary," Carla said to Sam. "I want Eve to fill me in on how the auction went."

"It went really well —" Eve began after the men had left.

"Forget the auction. What's going on between you and Daniel?"

Eve could feel the color creeping up into her cheeks and silently cursed the fair skin that betrayed her every feeling. "Nothing."

"Nothing?"

"We only just met," she said, wishing she didn't sound so defensive. "At the auction."

"I've seen that kind of 'nothing' before. Like when Sam and I met."

Eve knew enough of Carla and Sam's courtship to understand what her friend meant. It had had its share of ups and downs. But Carla was way off base now. There was nothing between herself and Daniel. There couldn't be.

Carla appeared to choose her words with care. "Daniel's a good man. A dedicated one."

"I know."

The sigh in Eve's voice must have gotten through to her friend, for Carla changed subjects.

They spent the next few minutes discussing the purely female details of giving birth. "It was incredible," Carla concluded. "And am I ever glad it's over."

When Sam and Daniel returned, Carla exchanged a quick glance with Sam, who nodded. Eve caught enough in that brief interchange to sense that Sam had been asking Daniel the same questions Carla had asked Eve.

Great, just great. Now their friends thought there was something between Daniel and herself.

Daniel saw the silent interrogation between husband and wife. From the questions Sam had asked, it wasn't hard to deduce that Carla had subjected Eve to the same gentle pumping for information. Daniel hid a smile. So he had some allies. He figured that with Eve, he'd need all the help he could get.

They spent several minutes admiring Zachary Samuel Hastings at the nursery window. Outside, Daniel took her arm and walked her to her car. "I didn't make the connection at first. Eve Dalton. Your mother was Evelyn Dalton."

She nodded.

He'd known of Evelyn Dalton, of course, though he'd never met her. A senator from Pennsylvania, her name had been tossed about as the running mate for the party's candidate for the top seat in the nation. An assassin's bullet had claimed her life before she'd given her acceptance. Daniel had just started his first year at Stanford. That had been nearly fifteen years ago. Eve couldn't have been more than a child then.

He remembered pictures of the young senator. She had vibrated life and energy and enthusiasm. Just as Eve did. "You favor her."

Memories of her mother danced like a phantom across her heart. She shook them away. "My mother was beautiful."

He skimmed a finger along her cheek. "So are you."

"Trying to score points, Senator?" A hard note edged her voice.

The tightening of his lips was the only sign that he'd acknowledged her hit.

"I'm only stating the facts."

She felt churlish and small. The fact was, talking about her mother was a pleasure and a pain that still had the power to cause her heart to tighten. Though she'd struggled to hold onto them, she had only scattered memories of her mother now, sprinkled across the years like so many bright beads torn from a broken strand.

"Someday maybe you'll trust me enough to tell me why you're so determined to keep me at arm's length."

"What's the matter, Senator? Haven't

you ever been rejected before?"

"No."

The simple arrogance of the word had a smile nudging at her lips. "Senator —"

"Daniel."

"Daniel, I've already told you my feelings about dating politicians."

"Don't you ever live dangerously?"

"Sure. I take risks all the time." Her voice hushed, she said, "I don't always floss after I brush. Once I even tore the tag off a pillow. You know, the one that says, 'Don't remove under penalty of law.' " She looked around. "Don't let it get out."

His voice equally low, he said, "I won't."

"I knew you could be trusted."

"Even if I'm a politician?"

"Even if you're a politician."

And she meant it. He radiated integrity and a simple goodness that was too frequently missing from figures in public life. Regret sharpened her voice as she hardened her heart to say what needed to be said. "Good-bye, Senator."

He ignored that. "Have dinner with me tonight." At her silence, he urged, "I'm only trying to get to know you better. Any harm in that?"

"No harm," she said at last. "As long as you don't mind getting turned down."

"I'm a patient man." He gave her time to digest the implications of his words before taking himself off.

Zachary Samuel Hastings let out a piercing wail, bringing the visiting minister's remarks to a close.

Chuckles could be heard from the congregation, with a loud Amen coming from Ethan Sandberg.

Carla whispered something to the minister, who nodded.

"Who stands up for this child?" he asked.

"We do," Eve and Daniel said in unison.

The reverend led the gathering in prayer. The ceremony completed, he gestured for the people to congratulate the new family.

Moved by the simple ceremony and the promises she'd made as Zachary's godmother, Eve searched for a tissue in her purse.

"Let me." Gently, Daniel took his own handkerchief and dabbed at the tears that stained her cheeks.

"Thanks." She sniffled. "Seems like we've done this before."

"Seems like."

Carla and Sam invited Eve and Daniel along with the entire congregation of

Carla's church to their home for a celebration party.

The church ladies, headed by Mrs. Miller, had outdone themselves. They bore casseroles and cupcakes. Pot roast and pies. Soups and salads.

Zachary occupied the center of attention. Apparently enjoying his role, he cooed and gurgled as he was fussed over.

With a promise to Carla to help in the kitchen, Eve made sure the platters of food remained full and clean dishes were available. When it appeared that everyone had been served, she joined the others in the front room.

"They make a beautiful family," a voice murmured at her side. Daniel's arm slipped around her.

Because he echoed her sentiments exactly, she stayed where she was.

"Do you want that?" he asked.

Her glance shifted to where Carla held Zach on her shoulder with Sam standing beside them, his hand fitted to the small of her back, the gesture both protective and tender. "With the right person," she answered.

"Do you have anyone in mind?"

The question was provocative, as he intended it to be, she guessed. She did the only smart thing and ignored it. Sharing the duties of godparent with Daniel Cameron was the last thing she had expected. How was she supposed to avoid him when they were thrown together at every opportunity?

"I have to go," she said.

"Have to or want to?"

"Right now, they're the same thing." She slipped away from the hand that still rested at her waist and made her way over to Carla and Sam. After saying her goodbyes, she left. She half expected Daniel to try and stop her, but he remained where he was.

The niggling sense of disappointment she experienced on the way home had nothing to do with him, she assured herself. It was a natural letdown after a full day.

That evening, she watched television and tried not to think about a man with serious eyes and a mouth that could turn up at the corners at the least provocation.

Her lack of success was measured by the way she sat through her favorite Hepburn-Tracy movie without realizing what she was watching. By the time the closing credits showed on the screen, she knew she was in trouble.

Chapter Three

The beauty of owning her own shop was freedom. Eve understood herself well enough to know she couldn't have tolerated working for someone else. Not that she minded taking orders. Well, maybe she did, just a little, she admitted in a spurt of honesty.

It was a matter of choice. As the sole proprietor, she could choose what she would make, what she would keep for herself, what she would sell. She set her own hours and created her own atmosphere.

It was a heady feeling, knowing the success — or failure — of her business depended upon no one but herself. She reveled in the knowledge and in the responsibility. If it became overwhelming sometimes, she recognized that the pressure would ease eventually.

She closed her shop promptly at five. She might spend the evenings spinning or experimenting with dyes, but she'd decided from the outset that she wouldn't be a slave to her business. The merchant in her demanded that she keep regular hours; the artist in her required she take time to dream.

Dreaming fed her soul. Without it, she would lose the essence of herself. And that would destroy whatever it was that made her work unique.

The best move she'd made was hiring Ron Franks. She'd met him through the mentor program sponsored by the local high school. He'd worked out so well that she'd made him assistant manager within a month, giving her time to take an hour or so off when it suited her mood.

Some might call her undisciplined. She knew better. Her work was important to her. So was her play. She was smart enough to understand that one enhanced the other. Without both, she wouldn't feel whole.

She could work at her spinning for twenty-four hours straight and then crash for the next twenty-four. The need to create didn't adhere to a schedule. Or she might keep to an eight-hour workday for weeks at a time without feeling stifled. Creation, like life itself, operated at its own cycle. She had accepted hers and didn't feel obligated to apologize for it. Her way might not work for some, but it allowed her the freedom she needed.

Ron worked every day after school and all day Saturday. She paid him well and encouraged him with his art. The arrangement suited them both. Ron had quickly become more than an employee, and she knew she'd miss him when he graduated next year and started college.

The service auction would go a long way toward providing scholarships for Ron and kids like him who were long on talent and short on money. Apparently she wasn't the only one who recognized his gift. Ron's art teacher had already approached Eve about writing a letter of recommendation for him when the time came to apply to college.

When the shop's doorbell sounded, she muttered something rude. An idea for a floor-length vest with matching tunic and pants had teased her brain all day, and she was just now putting it to paper. She wasn't above ignoring interruptions, but tonight something moved her to cross the room and open the door.

"You."

Daniel Cameron stood there. Impossibly handsome in jeans and a T-shirt, he looked as far removed from a United States senator as it was possible to be. As she'd guessed, his casual clothes didn't detract from his looks. On the contrary, they enhanced his attractiveness.

"Can I come in?" he asked when she continued to stare at him.

She thought about shutting the door in his face and decided against it. He looked quite capable of forcing his way in. Besides, she found that she wanted company.

Not that he was her first choice, she told herself. But he was handy.

She opened the door wider and took a step back.

"I needed to see you." With one long stride, he was but a scant inch from her. His nearness, combined with the frank admission, made the heat pop out on her cheeks.

He didn't follow up the remark with another, and she relaxed fractionally.

He looked about. Because she was a sucker for anyone who was interested in her craft, she showed him around. The colors and the textures were a part of her. She was vain enough to want others to appreciate them, philosophical enough to realize that many wouldn't.

She waited. Oddly, Daniel's reaction mattered. She refused to worry about why and held her breath as he fingered a particularly vividly colored jacket. Done in indigos and purples, with slashes of turquoise, it wouldn't appeal to everyone. She found her normally calm hands restless and linked them together to keep them still.

"Beautiful," he murmured. His fingers continued to caress the garment, but his gaze rested on her.

She resisted the urge to fuss with her hair. She'd started the day with her long hair twisted on top of her head in a casual arrangement of curls. Heat and work had sent it tumbling down her face and neck in an array of wisps and waves that refused her efforts to tame it with a brush.

"It's one of my favorites," she confided.

"Is it for sale?" Price tags were conspicuous only by their absence.

Eve would go to the stake before admitting it, but she couldn't bear to attach prices to her creations. Instead, she sized up the potential customer and her feelings about the piece in question. She never overcharged, but neither did she undervalue her work. In the end, her system, though unprofessional, suited both her and her customers. No one ever complained about her unconventional pricing, and she was content to have her designs going to people who appreciated them.

The success of her system was borne out by profits that continued to amaze her. If anyone had told her four years ago when she'd started her business that she'd be this successful, she'd have laughed. Over the years, she'd dabbled in pottery, stained glass, and photography. All had held her interest for a few months before she grew restless and moved on to something different. That she'd shown talent for each wasn't enough to keep her attention. Once she'd mastered a craft, she soon became bored, eager to try something new.

Weaving and spinning had been the exception. Maybe it was the lure of the colors. Creating her own had appealed to her from the first. And the feel of the different textures — nubby and coarse contrasting with silky and smooth.

Aware that Daniel was waiting, she said, "We're closed."

"Maybe you'd make an exception." Taking her hand in his, he traced the fine veins visible through the fair skin on the underside of her wrist.

Her pulse leaped, then steadied. She tried to concentrate on what he was saying rather than on the feelings he was arousing within her. "Maybe." Gently, she freed her hand. "Did you have someone special in mind?"

"Carla. I brought the baby Wilbert, but I figured she'd like something for herself."

Because Eve had always felt that new mothers needed extra pampering and attention, she felt herself warming to him. The man showed a sensitivity she hadn't credited him with. That part of her that softened toward him would never be able to harden again. "It's yours." Briskly, she removed the garment from the hanger and placed it in a gift box. Within minutes, it was wrapped with hand-stenciled paper, a bow fashioned of her own spun yarn topping it.

"How much?" he asked.

She chewed on her lip before naming a price. She'd lose money on it, but that didn't matter. What mattered was that the jacket was going to a friend.

He raised his eyebrows, but said nothing. Drawing a checkbook from his pocket, he filled out a check and handed it to her.

Without glancing at it, she rang up the sale and put it in the cash register.

"Have you had dinner yet?" he asked.

"I was going to throw together a salad." She thought of the head of limp lettuce in her refrigerator and grimaced. Salads were for rabbits, her father had frequently maintained.

"A woman who likes food as much as you do is settling for a salad?" He grabbed her hand. "Come on." When she hesitated, he gave her a shrewd look, "Or are you afraid?"

He knew, darn him. He knew she couldn't resist a challenge. Besides, she didn't really want to be alone. She was in the mood for conversation.

He held out his hands to his sides, palms up. "You can call the shots."

She considered. Just because she didn't date politicians didn't mean she had to deny herself a pleasant evening. And the promise of a good meal. The rationalization — oh, yes, she recognized it for what it was — caused her to smile. As long as she knew it, she'd be fine. "Give me five minutes to change."

Daniel explored the shop. He figured he had fifteen minutes, maybe thirty, before she returned. No woman of his acquaintance took only five minutes to change clothes.

Her shop was a reflection of the woman herself. Color and texture, energy and rich scents that he discovered came from a simmering pot of potpourri. Unexpected flashes of humor and bits of whimsy —

who else would have stationed a ceramic cocker spaniel standing guard at the door — mingled comfortably with one-of-a-kind garments.

The shop was another bit of the puzzle of the woman who continued to intrigue him more each time he saw her.

He was learning. It was a mistake to try to anticipate this woman, to try to predict her reaction to any given situation. She was like no woman he'd ever known.

She owned a business, stocked it with her own designs, and still managed to find time to help disadvantaged teenagers. She knew the business of politics, could hold her own in a society party, and had walked away from a world many considered the quintessence of glamour and power.

It threw him. At first he'd tried to fit her into a slot. Then he realized Eve couldn't be categorized. She was her own person, content with who and what she was.

No wonder she'd baffled him at first. In Washington, everyone was so busy pretending to be more than they were. With Eve, what you saw was what you got. A warm, vibrant woman who knew what she wanted and wasn't afraid to go after it.

When she reappeared within the stated time, he could only stare. She wore a long, cream-colored skirt paired with a matching blouse, both out of some soft, flowing material. Her only jewelry was a heavy gold pendant.

"Yours?" he asked, unable to resist touching the finely woven cloth that draped across her shoulders.

She nodded.

"I like it."

That drew a smile from her, and she slipped her arm in his. "Where are we going? Someplace wildly expensive with lots of atmosphere and menus you need a translator to understand?"

He kept his smile under wraps. "You'll see."

The restaurant had always been one of his favorites. Tucked between two high-rise office buildings, it was an anachronism. The owner had received offers over the years to sell what had become a prime piece of real estate, but, to the relief of his loyal patrons, he'd always refused.

Wooden tables sported oilcloths and plain dishes and cutlery. The only outstanding feature of the place was the food. Hot and plenty, it was devoid of fancy sauces with fancy names. He wondered what Eve would think of it.

Daniel ordered the chicken-fried steak.

After studying the menu, Eve chose the Yankee pot roast. He watched as she glanced around the room. He felt a flash of satisfaction that he'd managed to surprise her. Her expression told him she'd expected him to take her to a slick, trendy place that was long on ambience and short on good food.

Surprising her hadn't been his intent on bringing her here. He'd suffered through too many rubber chicken dinners at political fund-raisers to choose a restaurant for anything other than the quality of its food. But if he'd succeeded in throwing Eve a curve, so much the better. The lady was entirely too smug with her opinions about politicians in general and him in particular. He planned to change her mind. At least about one senator.

He reached across the table to take her hand in his.

"You were surprised when I said I'd come tonight," she said. The self-satisfied tone had his grin come out from where it had been hiding.

"No."

The chagrin on her face drew a chuckle from him, which he hastily turned into a cough.

"Why not?"

"Because I knew you couldn't resist a dare."

She smiled faintly, apparently recovered from her bout of pique that she'd failed to surprise him. "A dare. Why, Senator, I thought you relied on your charm."

"Even senators have their limitations. So, why *did* you agree to come?"

Her laugh was rich and full of the fun she poked at herself. "I can't resist a dare."

He turned her hand over, studying the fragile lines of it, the long, clever fingers, nicked and scratched from her work, he guessed. "Any other reason you said yes?"

Gently, she disengaged her hand. "A woman's got to eat."

Remembering the amount of food she'd put away at the auction, he wondered if that were her primary reason for coming. "Please," he said, clutching his chest dramatically and earning a smile from her. "Don't bolster my ego. I don't think I could stand any more flattery."

The waiter reappeared then, temporarily halting the conversation.

The food was as good as he remembered, the portions generous, and the company stimulating. Eve talked knowledgeably about foreign affairs one moment and the next was passionately defending the rights of animals. She was as unpredictable in her opinions as she was in her choice of clothes. Her convictions might not always be politically correct — he grimaced at the term — but they were delivered with an intensity that made the listener sit up and take notice.

She was both rational and intelligent, emotional and passionate. He was discovering that both sides appealed to him. She was nothing like the society women he normally dated. She could charm one minute and offend the next, all without missing a beat.

"Tell me about this scholarship fund," he invited.

Always eager to talk about her favorite project, she launched into a description of what the scholarship program could be to a dozen children. She stopped, her eyes narrowing in an assessing glance. "You already knew all this, didn't you?"

He shrugged. "I did a little research today."

"Then why ask me?"

"I had the facts. I wanted more. What I couldn't find in a bunch of reports." He covered her hand with his own. "You really care about the kids, don't you?"

"Yes," she said softly. "I do."

He'd known, of course, that she'd undercharged him for the gift for Carla and guessed at the reason. That she hadn't even bothered to glance at the check he'd handed her amused and exasperated him by turns. How did she expect to stay in business when she practically gave away her merchandise? He'd like to be around when she discovered that he'd ignored the ridiculously low price she'd named and paid what he hoped was a fair value for the garment.

On second thought, maybe it'd be just as well if he wasn't present then. He had a feeling the lady's temper was as unpredictable as her conversation.

". . . they just need a chance." She paused for a breath. "What do you think?" she asked, drawing him back to the present.

"About what?"

"Aha." Her look of triumph had a smile sliding across his lips. "I knew you weren't listening."

"Guilty," he confessed. "I was wondering how you stayed in business when you give away your work."

"I don't . . ." She stopped, then frowned. "It's my business. I have a right to set my own prices. Besides, it was for a friend."

"Is that what we are? Friends?"

"I was speaking of Carla," she said

primly, but a smile peeked out anyway, encouraging him to ask the question that he'd been wanting to ask all evening.

"What about us?"

He'd thought she might laugh it off or possibly give a glib answer like "There is no us."

All traces of humor vanished from her eyes. "Daniel, I like you . . ." She hadn't meant to say that. He knew it by the look of chagrin that crossed her face.

"Good. We're making progress."

"You don't give up, do you?"

"Not when it comes to something I want." The words were said lightly, but his eyes held a promise.

Her quick intake of breath told him she understood.

The challenge had been issued.

And accepted.

He took her home early, content with what he'd accomplished tonight. She wasn't indifferent to him. He was satisfied. For now.

At her front door, she took out her keys and unlocked it. He didn't expect to be asked in. Not yet. He'd say good night and go.

However, when she turned to him with a thank-you on her lips and gratitude in her eyes, all his good intentions scattered like confetti tossed by the wind.

He moved closer. He heard — or felt — the quick hitch of her heart. He lowered his head. When he touched his lips to hers, hers parted on a soft sigh.

His fingers curled around her upper arms, urging her closer. When he lifted his head, he imagined that her eyes glowed warmly. It was too dark to see her face, but he felt the heat from her blush. Or maybe it was the heat of his own skin. Right now, they were so close it was hard to tell.

Another sigh shuddered from her, a soft ripple of sound that cut straight to his heart.

"Good night, Senator," she said and gently closed the door behind her.

Daniel knew he'd made a mistake. He'd rushed her. He'd known it when he kissed her. He'd known it when she trembled in his arms. He'd known it, and still he'd gone ahead.

Her fear hurt. He had yet to discover why. Why was she so skittish around him? It was all part of the puzzle, a puzzle he was determined to put together. The one thing he knew for sure was that he didn't intend on giving up.

A steady stream of customers the following day kept Eve busy, but not too busy to think.

Daniel. He'd crossed her mind a dozen times during the day. Okay, it was only noon now. She multiplied twelve by the number of hours left in the day and groaned.

She wouldn't put up with it. She'd push him out of her thoughts, out of her dreams, out of her life. That resolved, she felt better.

And she succeeded. She managed to get through the afternoon and the evening with never a thought of him. Okay, an errant thought might have slipped past her resolve. Stray images of the way his dark brown hair slipped across his forehead, of the sudden flashes of humor that touched his eyes, of the warm taste of his lips, might have found their way into her mind.

Since she'd been thinking about him for the better part of the day, she shouldn't have been surprised when he appeared at her door that evening.

"Can I come in?" Daniel asked.

She gestured him inside. The room seemed to shrink, his presence eating up the up-until-now adequate space. With the shrinkage of the room went a loss of air, and she struggled to breathe.

"I wanted to apologize," he said. "For last night."

"You don't have to —"

"That's where you're wrong. I promised I'd take things easy. I broke that promise. That's not something I'm proud of, not something I usually do."

She believed that. He was a politician, yes, but he was also a man of integrity. She'd sensed that within minutes of meeting him.

"I'm sorry," he said.

She was unsure of her response. Because she wasn't sorry. She wasn't sorry at all.

He leaned against the wall. "We need to talk."

"About what?"

"Dating."

"Dating?" The air in the room seemed to evaporate again.

"Dating. As in a man and a woman who are attracted to each other, seeing each other, going out, having fun."

"I told you —"

"We'll take it slow." He held up a hand as if he anticipated her response. "I promise. Slow and easy. You set the pace."

Something in his tone didn't give her a choice. And she realized she didn't *want* to refuse. Heaven help her, she wanted to spend time with him.

"Okay," she said, hating the breathless, tentative note in her voice, hating the weakness in her knees, hating the blush she could feel stain her cheeks. Trying to hate him — and failing — because he knew her better than she knew herself.

The relief she saw in his eyes told her he wasn't half as casual about the whole thing as she had first supposed. And that gave her confidence. Her breath steadied, her knees straightened, she was in control once more.

That hard-won control scattered at his next words, like dust motes caught in a summer breeze.

"I like flirting with you. And I really like the way you blush." He skimmed a finger down her cheek.

As expected, Eve blushed. Again.

The man was entirely too sure of himself, entirely too attractive, entirely too everything for a woman's peace of mind.

One beat of her heart tripped madly over the next, the rhythm picking up and destroying her short-lived confidence. She felt strange, shimmery, and very much alive. All because a man told her he liked flirting with her, liked the way she blushed. Not just any man, she silently amended. One man in particular.

How was she supposed to combat the kind of appeal he gave off so effortlessly? How was she supposed to keep her sanity when one look from him, one touch, sent her over the edge?

"Will you see me tomorrow night?" he asked.

Thinking with her heart — no, that wasn't right, she wasn't thinking at all — she agreed.

Daniel struggled over where to take Eve. The knowledge annoyed him. He, who was known for his definitive decision-making, couldn't make up his mind on such a simple matter. Eve had done that to him. She'd turned him inside out and upside down. That she'd done it without even trying only added to his irritation.

In the end, he decided on a Native American exhibit at a local art gallery, reasoning that there was bound to be a crowd, which would forestall any chance of intimacy. He regretted that. But his first concern was putting her at ease.

Slow and easy would be his hallmarks, though his every instinct urged him to declare his feelings, to convince her that what they had together was too special, too rare to be ignored. But it was too soon.

Chapter Four

Eve slipped into a long vest and matching skirt, fashioned out of silky yarn. She twisted her hair in an intricate knot at the nape of her neck and secured it with a pearl clip. Daniel had told her to pull out all the stops in dressing but had refused to tell her where he was taking her.

A dozen times she'd picked up the phone to call him and cancel. A dozen times she'd replaced it. She stepped outside. Perhaps the cool air would clear away the cobwebs that had taken up residence in her mind.

Stars spangled the sky. Candles in heaven's windows, Carla had once told her. Looking at the glittering night, Eve believed it. The night promised magic. The only question was, did she want to share it with Daniel?

Yes.

The answer came so swiftly that she had no time to doubt it. How could the wrong man feel so right?

When Daniel materialized out of the darkness, she took a step back. "I didn't hear you drive up," she said, hating the breathless note in her voice.

"You were too busy stargazing."

Without a word, she put her hand in his.

Two nights ago he'd disarmed her with a quiet evening at a local café. Tonight she expected him to try to dazzle her with dinner at a five-star restaurant.

Once more he'd succeeded in surprising her. When they arrived at an art gallery, she hardly dared believe it.

"I thought you might enjoy this," he said, taking her evening wrap and checking it at the door.

She looked about at the people dressed in their finery. Invitations to the gallery's Native American show were practically impossible to come by. She'd tried and failed to secure one. Now she was here.

The exhibit was magnificent.

Hammered copper belts, turquoise and silver squash blossom necklaces, brightly woven blankets, and beaded leather dresses were only the beginning. She ignored the hovering waiters with their trays of champagne; she didn't need the artificial high. She was already high — high on the display of beauty before her.

She hurried between one display and another, anxious to see, to touch, to experience everything.

A hand on her arm halted her rush. She looked up to find Daniel grinning at her.

"Slow down," he said. "It's not going anywhere."

Impulsively, she hugged him. "Thank you."

"You're welcome."

"How did you know?"

"I didn't. I hoped." Not giving her a chance to reply, he kissed the tip of her nose and steered her toward a collection of pottery.

The simple designs held a classic grace that she found instantly appealing. Her own attempts at pottery had produced adequate results, perhaps even more than adequate, but they lacked the classic elegance she saw before her now.

"They're beautiful," she breathed.

"You're beautiful."

His words stayed with her for the rest of the evening. When he took her home, she invited him in.

Eve unlocked the door and, for the first time she could remember, wished she'd spent a few minutes straightening up her home before she left. Her housekeeping skills — or lack of them — had never bothered her before. Instinctively, she knew Daniel's home would reflect the same orderliness that he brought to the rest of his life.

She angled her chin. She wasn't one to waste her time on regrets. Besides, it wasn't like she wanted to impress the man. That was the last thing she wanted, she assured herself. The last thing.

Still, she found herself kicking a shoe under the sofa as she walked through the living room.

"Hey, you don't have to clean up on my account."

"Okay, so I'm not the happy homemaker."

"I always believed you could tell a lot about a person by where they live."

"Okay. I'll bite."

"You love books."

"So you've got twenty-twenty eyesight," she said with a glance at the floor-to-ceiling bookshelves that lined a full wall. "What else?"

"You put people above things." He slanted her a knowing glance. "How am I doing?"

"Not bad."

"You surround yourself with color."

"Colors are my business."

"They're more than that." He touched the multicolored shawl that fastened at her waist. "They're part of you."

She took a step back.

His perception was unnerving. Yet one more piece of evidence that he knew her better than she wanted to admit. For the sake of her sanity, she had to keep her distance. Her heart, though, urged her to close the space she'd so recently created. Her heart won the struggle.

Daniel took the choice from her as one step ate up the space between them. He was now but a heartbeat away. She guessed his intent as he lowered his head. She could have objected, could have moved. She did neither. Instead, she waited for the kiss she knew would make the world stop.

When the kiss came, she was ready.

Or so she thought.

The kiss was light and quick. Surely, it wasn't enough to send sparks snapping down her nerve ends. Yet that's what happened. Warmth suffused her as she melted into his embrace.

She'd forgotten. All she knew for one wonderful moment was that she was being held in strong arms, by a man who made her feel very much a woman. When memory — and reality — returned, she pulled away, her breath coming in rapid puffs.

Reality slammed into her, and she took a step backward. Daniel was a politician, everything she'd sworn to stay away from. His smiles shouldn't make her pulse race faster or her heart do somersaults.

When he kissed her again, she knew she hadn't been mistaken. If anything, she'd underestimated his effect on her. The world didn't just stop; it tilted off its axis before coming to that stop.

With his lips centered on hers, she was grounded. She needed no other support. Still, her hands moved to his shoulders, then around his neck. So close were they that she couldn't tell where her heartbeat stopped and his started. And she knew this was what she'd been waiting for all her life.

She knew she was playing with fire, knew he was taking her heart places she wasn't ready to go, knew she should put an end to it.

"You promised," she reminded him, wishing she didn't sound so breathless, that her heart didn't pound like a sledgehammer in her chest.

"So I did." He drew in a shuddering

breath, as if he, too, had been shaken to the core. Then he took himself off, out the door, leaving her to stare after him.

Beautiful. He'd called her beautiful. Had he really meant it? Or was he one of those men who handed out compliments as easily as they breathed? Somehow she didn't think so.

Annoyed at herself for even thinking about it, she shook her head. She didn't want to feel pleased at his compliments. He'd be here a week, two at the most, and then leave for Washington. She didn't want to feel anything but relief when he disappeared from her life.

Then why did this attraction to him persist? The question plagued her into the night, disrupting her sleep and turning her dreams into nightmares.

No, not nightmares, she scrupulously reminded herself in the morning. No dream that held Daniel Cameron looking at her with those serious gray eyes could be called a nightmare.

Eve had learned early in life not to pin too much on dreams, especially if those dreams depended upon other people. Still, a few secret hopes that she'd hugged in the secret places of her heart persisted, undiminished by the realities of life.

The next morning, pushing away the memories, she concentrated on updating her books. Accounting wasn't one of her strengths. For that reason, she was determined to master it. When the books balanced, she gave a relieved sigh.

Her mind unoccupied, her thoughts returned to Daniel. She'd always hoped that someday she would meet a man who would stir her in a way too powerful to resist, too commanding to ignore.

So why was she thinking of that now? That she'd recently met Daniel Cameron had no bearing on it. None at all, she assured herself. It was coincidence. Nothing more.

She didn't *want* to be breathless around him, to feel weak-kneed and tingly just because he was near. She didn't want to, but she did.

Spending the evenings with Eve was becoming a habit. A very pleasurable habit, Daniel thought with a smile. He hadn't expected to be able to get away tonight. Meetings with local party members normally lasted far into the night. That this one hadn't was a bonus, one he hoped to share with Eve.

When he knocked at her door, no one

answered. The shop door was unlocked, and he pushed it open. He walked through the kitchen on his way to the workshop.

Jasmine and lavender. She'd taught him enough for him to recognize the scents that greeted him. With bunches of weeds hanging from the ceiling and a pot of herbs simmering on the stove, it resembled an old-fashioned apothecary. The smile that touched his lips was one of tenderness. She'd made herself a nest here, full of colors and scents and textures, as far removed from his Washington town house as it was possible to be.

Strange. He felt at home here. The style wasn't one he'd have chosen for himself. His tastes ran more to classic lines, the smell of leather, the feel of rich fabrics. He'd carved out a place for himself amid the tinsel and phoniness that composed so much of the nation's capital.

But that didn't mean he couldn't admire what Eve had managed to do here. The small room didn't look contrived but somehow right. It suited her.

The kitchen opened into the workshop. From his vantage point, he saw Eve. Involved in her task, she didn't look up. He stared, transfixed. It wasn't the room that drew him now but the woman inside it. A

Madonna-like smile changed her features from animated to thoughtful.

Was she thinking of him?

The idea had his lips curving upward. His ego was as out of control as Eve had claimed if he believed that. More likely, she was thinking of a new design.

She sat in the middle of the floor, legs tucked under her, hair a wild mane of red and gold, haloing her face. In her lap she held a skein of yarn, the deep purple contrasting sharply with the fair skin of her hands.

Over and over, she wound the yarn, her motions as graceful as those of a ballerina. He watched, fascinated. Light played across her face, shifting as the breeze stirred the curtains which filtered it.

The serenity of her pose, the absolute peace that radiated off her in waves held him rooted to the spot. It was more than beauty, although she had that in abundance. It was an inner harmony that said she knew who she was and was content with it.

His hands fisted at his sides as he admitted that he could destroy that peace. Not willingly. Never that. But he knew himself well enough to recognize that what he felt for her wasn't going to go away.

This was the real thing, the forever-and-ever kind of love that poets revered and composers exalted.

He wished he had the fancy words to tell her of his feelings, the talent to put them to music. All he had was a heart that belonged to her.

Her hands moved with an unconscious grace and again he was reminded of a dancer. He took pleasure in the act of watching her. For now, he was content simply to watch. But not forever, he promised himself.

Not forever.

She felt him. It wasn't something she could define. No sound or movement had given him away. It was the presence that made him who he was. She could understand the voters' infatuation with him. He exuded power, a quiet strength that invited trust. How could she deny what was so plainly evident?

She lifted her head and smiled. "You're supposed to be in a meeting."

"Disappointed?"

"No."

"Good. Because I couldn't stay away."

His honesty didn't surprise her. She knew him well enough to understand that he didn't play games. It was something else she appreciated. She'd had enough of the game-playing that was part and parcel of the political scene in the nation's capital.

Daniel crossed the room to her, drawing her back to the present. She scrambled to her feet and placed her hands on his shoulders. He felt big and solid beneath her touch, a man a woman could count on, a man she could feel safe with.

The direction of her thoughts had her pulling back. She had admitted him into her life, but that didn't mean she was going to allow him any further. Her heart was out of bounds. As long as she kept to that, she'd be all right. She had to be.

She started to pick up her yarn when he stopped her. "You don't have to be afraid."

That had her chin lifting. "I'm not."

"Good. Show me what you're doing."

"I'm getting ready to make a rug. This —" here she handed him the skein of yarn "— is one of the things I'll be weaving it out of." She tugged at his hand. "Come on back and I'll show you the rest."

Floor-to-ceiling shelves separated the work area from the living area. Bulky spools of thread and skeins of yarn filled every available space.

"Have you ever seen a loom before?" she asked.

"Only in pictures."

She pointed to the massive piece that occupied the center of the workroom. "This is a floor loom. The warp threads stretch from here to —" she pointed to the other side "— there. The heddles lift and lower the threads so that the weft threads can be slipped crosswise, over and under the warp ones."

He held up a hand. "Hey, slow down. You're talking to a man who doesn't know his right from his weft."

A sheepish smile inched across her lips. "Sorry. I tend to get carried away." She picked up a sheaf of papers and handed it to him. "Maybe this'll give you an idea of what I do."

He glanced through the papers, which turned out to be drawings. Watercolor sketches showed dresses, blouses, jackets, every imaginable type of clothing made from handwoven cloth. The colors were those of the earth and sky, ranging from the palest green of a young plant to a deep, rich brown of newly turned soil to the crimson of sunset.

He looked at her in surprise. "You're an artist."

"Some think so." Her lips curved up at the corners. "You thought I was just some nutcase playing with yarn. Right?"

This time it was his turn to smile sheepishly. "Never a nutcase."

"But a little strange," she persisted.

"Maybe a little."

"Okay, Senator. I'm some weirdo artist and you're a politician. Doesn't sound like the thing dreams are made of, does it?"

Beneath her tart tone was regret. He heard it and seized upon it. The lady didn't really want him to leave her alone. She felt this thing between them as surely as he did.

Now wasn't the time to pursue it. He turned his interest back to the sketches and swatches of cloth attached to them. What attracted him most was the feel of the material. It wasn't crisp to the touch, as commercially loomed cloth felt. It draped softly, as though it were made to caress the skin instead of simply covering it.

The fanciful direction of his thoughts had his lips edging upward. He'd never been one for a fancy turn of phrase. Contrary to popular opinion, not all politicians favored pretty words. His own bordered on plainness, at times, bluntness. It had taken the right woman to bring out the poetry he was told resided in every Scotsman's soul.

She placed her hands over his, gently guiding them to work the shuttle.

"You try it now."

It looked simple enough, but he wasn't fooled. He knew she had spent years perfecting her art. He wasn't arrogant enough to assume he could duplicate her work. But neither was he one to ignore a challenge.

He looked down as her long, slender hands deftly worked their magic on the yarn. His own felt clumsy and huge in comparison.

"You aren't paying attention," she accused.

But he was. Just not to the matter of weaving. He grinned before turning his focus back on what she was showing him. Her hands on his, she guided him through the motions.

"See?" she said when they'd successfully completed one line. "You did it."

What he saw was the pale skin of her hands resting atop the darkly tanned skin of his own. What he saw were two people, different from each other in so many ways, yet right in the most fundamental ones. What he saw was — he looked up to watch her animated face — the woman he wanted to spend the rest of his life with.

But he couldn't tell her that. Not yet.

The two words chafed at him, but he held onto his resolve. There'd be a time. Soon, if he had his way.

He looked tired, Eve thought with a quick pang of concern. Her worry about keeping her heart whole slipped away as she reached up to touch the lines of strain that formed grooves at the corners of his mouth and eyes.

Daniel found himself oddly soothed by the concern he read in her eyes. He was accustomed to the long hours his job demanded. Having someone worry about him was something new, though. He could get used to it, he decided.

"You look bushed."

"Right the first time." He rotated his shoulders, trying to ease the kinks that had him twisted up in knots.

"Let me."

He closed his eyes and felt her hands settle at the base of his neck. Her fingers tightened and dug deep. His first response was to scream in agony but the almost-scream died as his muscles slowly relaxed, turning to jelly. Waves of pleasure rippled outward from where her hands touched, seeping into every inch of his body.

Her hands settled between his shoulders

now, rubbing, kneading, coaxing the tension there to ease and, finally, disappear. Her fingers slid down his back, gently soothing away every ounce of tension, working their magic until he was all but purring.

"Mmmm. Anybody ever tell you that you've got magic fingers?"

She smiled at his nonsense. "Tell me what's got you so tied up in knots."

And he did. He talked. Without wondering how he sounded. Without worrying if he made sense. Without anything but the need to share what he was feeling.

"I want to make a difference. That's why I ran for office in the first place. I know a lot of people just think it's a family thing, but it's more. I want to make things better." He laughed shortly. "I can't believe I said that. It sounds unbelievably corny."

"Not to me."

"You really mean that, don't you?"

The sincerity in her eyes was answer enough.

He twisted around long enough to tuck a strand of hair behind her ear. "Thanks for listening. I didn't realize I needed that. Until now." His hand slipped to cup her chin. "You're easy to be with."

It was the nicest compliment she'd ever been given.

Her fingers continued to work their magic as she listened, and he felt much of the tension melt away as he talked. Sleep snuck up on him, and he gave in to the exhaustion that had dogged him all day.

An hour, then two, passed. Still, he slept. Eve worked at her loom, content that he was there. A frown worked its way between her brows as she thought of how tense he'd been when he arrived.

The responsibilities he carried would only multiply as he advanced in the party. And she knew he would. His need to serve, to make things better for the people of this country, would see to it.

Chapter Five

Daniel had a call to return to his Washington office, another to a party leader. But all he could think of was Eve. It had been three days since their last date. Three days in which he'd reminded himself that he'd promised to take things slow. Three days in which he'd kept that promise. Three days in which he'd tried to convince himself he didn't need to see her every night. Before he could talk himself out of it, he punched out her number.

"See me tonight?" he asked.

"Did it ever occur to you that you might try calling a lady in advance?"

He heard the "I'm-trying-not-to-smile-but-I-can't-help-myself" tone in her voice. "I might. But I didn't."

"What if I have other plans?" she asked, still with that trying-not-to-smile tone.

"Do you?"

"No. But that's not —"

"I'll pick you up at seven." He hung up without giving her a chance to refuse. His own smile was not of the trying-not-to type. It was an honest-to-goodness one, an if-I-died-now-I'd-die-happy one. It was the smile of a man in love.

Eve checked her watch. Again. Her breath fled entirely, along with all thought, as the chimes on the front door sounded. She'd have suffered the most horrible of tortures before admitting it, but she'd been waiting for this moment all day.

Daniel stood there, more handsome than any man had a right to be, more dear than her heart wanted to admit.

"What made you think I'd be here? Waiting?" she asked.

"Because you like me." One corner of his mouth tipped into a lopsided grin. The other followed suit, evening it out.

She felt her own lips imitate his. The man was incorrigible. His conceit was infectious. How could she resist him? The answer was simple: she couldn't.

She drew him into the kitchen and handed him a soda. "What did you do today?"

"Took some calls. Thought about you. Wrote a couple of letters. Thought about you some more. Had a meeting. Thought about you a lot. Drafted a response —"

Her smile spread like an awakening sunbeam. "I'm beginning to get the idea."

"Good." He bent to brush a kiss on the side of her neck. "Come on. We don't want to be late."

"Where are we going?" she asked, grabbing her jacket.

"You'll see."

The air was heavy with excitement, the aroma of butter-flavored oil poured over popcorn, and bodies pressed together.

The carnival.

She took in the sights and scents and sounds with the abandon of a child. Tugging on Daniel's hand, she dragged him from one ride to another. The Scrambler, Hoop-the-Hoop, Whirly Birds, they did them all. She clung to him for dear life as the tiny cup they were strapped into jerked and tumbled its way down the impossibly narrow tracks of the Wild Mouse.

He flexed his hand when they disembarked, drawing her attention to crescent-shaped grooves which scored his palm.

"Did I do that?" she asked.

" 'Fraid so, sweetheart." As she started to form an apology, he pulled her to him. "Hey, don't worry. It's a small price to pay for getting to hold hands with my best girl."

His words were light, but she wondered. Did he mean it? That part about her being his best girl? And how did she feel about it if he did? How did she *want* to feel about it? She had no time to ponder it, as he pulled her toward another ride.

A meager breeze ruffled his hair, and she reached up to smooth it off his forehead just as he did the same. Their hands collided. Dark against light. Hard against soft. Man against woman. He caught her fingers in his and laced them together.

Laughter spilled around them with the punctuation of shrill screams. Multicolored lights winked, beckoning the carnivalgoers to the sideshows — the fire-eating woman, the Gypsy palm reader, the hall of mirrors. For tonight, they weren't Senator Cameron and date but simply two people enjoying each other.

She realized that was all she wanted them to be. Two ordinary people with ordinary jobs doing ordinary things living ordinary lives. Ordinary — the one thing Daniel could never be.

The realization sobered her. Aware that he was watching her, she pushed the unsettling thoughts from her mind. Tonight belonged to them. Whatever happened, whatever didn't happen, they'd have tonight.

They feasted on pink cotton candy, hot dogs sloppy with ballpark-type mustard, washed down with giant paper cups of root beer.

"My stomach's not going to thank me for this tomorrow morning," she said, wiping mustard from her lips as she finished her second hot dog.

"You missed a spot." He took the napkin from her and dabbed at the corner of her mouth.

The gesture spoke of intimacy. It was then that a flash exploded in front of her eyes. If she hadn't just swallowed, she would have choked.

She blinked against the temporary blindness, groping for Daniel's hand.

He shielded her from further pictures, but the carefree mood was spoiled. They tried to recapture it. They laughed, but the laughter came too late. They held hands but felt self-conscious. How many other amateur photographers were out there, waiting to snap a picture of a United States senator out enjoying himself with a woman?

The ride home held none of the earlier

good spirits. At her house, he didn't wait for an invitation but came inside. They had to have this out before it festered.

"I'll make us some coffee," she said, starting toward the kitchen.

He followed her, watching as she went through the motions of making coffee, concentrating on covering the grounds with water, careful not to pour too much water, or too little. She caught her tongue between her teeth, a gesture he'd come to recognize. It meant that she was troubled.

He wanted to protest that he didn't want coffee, but he knew she needed time.

"It'll be ready in a few minutes," she said without turning around.

He took the hint, and headed back to the front room. He contented himself by looking around. The living room was a treasure trove, filled with both things Eve had created and things Eve loved. A cloisonné elephant shared space with a fragile Lladro figurine. Two woven wall hangings flanked a traditional landscape. A rag rug covered the plank floor. The effect was at once exciting, yet peaceful. Like pieces of a jigsaw puzzle, they fit together to form a whole.

When she returned, he took the tray from her and set it on a table. He turned her in his arms so that her back was to him. His arms linked around her waist, he rested his brow on the back of her head and sighed deeply. Having some enterprising photographer snap pictures of him was nothing out of the ordinary. To him.

To Eve, it was something else. He felt the tension in her, the struggle to control it. He'd prefer she yell, scream, give way to the anger he knew she was feeling, anything but this quiet.

She felt small and fragile in his arms. She was so vibrant, so full of energy and life that he sometimes forgot how vulnerable she really was.

"Let it out," he urged.

"It's nothing."

His patience snapped, and he made a rude sound. "You hated it. Admit it."

"All right. I hated it."

"Good." He let out a long breath. "Chances are it won't make the papers."

She nodded, but they both knew differently. Senator Daniel Cameron was news — whether in the amusement park or on the Senate floor.

They said stilted good-byes.

The hope that the picture would be ignored or buried on the back page vanished when she opened the morning paper.

There they were on the front page, with the caption: "Senator amuses himself at amusement park." Eve cringed at the coy wording. She read the brief, chatty article accompanying the picture.

The calls started that morning. By ten, she took the phone off the hook.

There was no reason for her to be upset, she reminded herself. The paper hadn't printed anything that wasn't true. She *was* seeing a United States senator. The hint that there was something more between them than simple friendship was only a standard gossip columnist ploy.

She and Daniel shared common friends; it was only natural that a friendship should develop between the two of them. *Yeah.* And if she believed that, maybe she ought to buy some swampland in Florida.

Was that the real reason for her distress? That she knew her feelings for Daniel went far beyond friendship?

Everything had changed. She was too aware of him. Of how he made her feel. She could no longer pretend that their relationship was one of simple friendship.

Daniel was beginning to mean far too much to her. *Get real,* she ordered herself angrily. He already did. She'd known it from the beginning, hadn't she? That she could care for him . . . she refused to think beyond that.

So what did she do?

Absently, she picked up a skein of heather-colored yarn.

She approached the problem as she would a knot in a tangled ball of yarn. Normally, she would gently tug at the yarn, first one way, then another until the knot finally loosened. A final tug and it would give way. No matter how she tried to unsnarl the twisted pieces of herself and Daniel, though, she could see no way to reconcile their differences. It wasn't that they saw the world through differently colored glasses; they weren't even looking at the same world.

She picked up the knotted skein, the strands hopelessly enmeshed in each other. And if the knot failed to unravel? Well, then, she had no choice but to cut it out. Slowly, she picked up her scissors. The nearly silent snip mocked what she knew she had to do.

Somehow, she knew that cutting Daniel from her life would be far more painful.

When he arrived that evening, he didn't have to wonder what her reaction to the article in the paper had been. It was there on her face.

"You saw it?"

"Yeah." She flipped the paper over casually, covering the picture.

She was upset. He could see it in her eyes, hear it in what she hadn't said.

"I'm sorry." He reached out and let his fingers glide down the satin of her cheek.

"It's not your fault." She twirled a curl around her finger. "It must be hard living in a fishbowl."

"You get used to it."

"Do you?" She picked up a vase, set it down again, and reached for a book.

He stilled her restless hands in his. "Why don't you let me take you out? We'll go for a drive and —"

"It doesn't matter. Don't you see? You're news. Wherever you go, whatever you do, someone will be there waiting, wanting a piece of you."

"It's not that bad."

"I won't let it happen to me. Not again."

"You're letting something that happened years ago control your life." He had to reach her somehow. Maybe cruelty could accomplish what understanding had failed to. "I thought you were stronger than that."

She looked as though he'd slapped her, but then she slipped on the mask that he knew she pulled out only when she was upset. Or scared. "You're entitled to your opinion." The uppity tone would normally have had him smiling, but he heard the pain, the fear that layered the words.

"What I'm entitled to is the truth."

"You want the truth, Senator? Try this. I don't want a relationship with you. Not now. Not ever. You pushed your way into my life, and I gave in. But I'm calling it quits. My choice. My right."

"Your choice. Your right. What about my choices, my rights? I . . . care about you." He might as well say the rest of it. "I haven't felt this way about a woman in a long time. Maybe never." He waited for her reaction to his admission, one that had surprised him, not by the words themselves but by the intensity with which he'd uttered them.

"I know. But I can't care for you."

"You already do."

It wasn't arrogance on his part since he'd spoken only the truth. She *did* care. More than she'd believed possible.

"Daniel, I'm sorry. I can't see you again."

"You don't want to see me again."

He didn't know how much she wanted to. Self-preservation kept her steadfast, despite the accusation in his eyes. "I can't."

She reached up to skim her knuckles

down his jaw. The gesture was one of good-bye.

"Okay." Not a hint of sarcasm colored his words; not a glint of mischief sparked his eyes.

She stared at him, waiting for the relief she was sure would come. It didn't.

He was serious. He didn't intend on calling her, coming by to see her, bullying her into accepting dates — everything she'd claimed she wanted. She would be able to have her life back again, secure in the knowledge that Daniel Cameron wouldn't be coming around anymore, making outrageous suggestions, tempting her with what couldn't be.

She ought to be jumping for joy, planning a celebration. She ought to be doing all those things and more. Then why did she feel so depressed?

Daniel walked out the door. And out of her life.

A meeting with Sam Hastings about the homeless problem in Saratoga forced Daniel to focus on something other than Eve. Or it should have.

"What's up?" Sam asked when he had to repeat a question a couple of times before Daniel took it in. "Your mind's obviously somewhere, but it's not here."

Daniel dredged up a semblance of a smile. "A certain redhead."

Sam's grin was gleefully unsympathetic. "What's Eve done?"

"Refused to see me."

"Ohhhhhh."

Daniel gave his friend a sour look. "Yeah." His lips tightened. "The lady's due for a surprise."

Sam's expression sobered. "Just be sure you know what you're doing. Eve's a great person. She's also vulnerable."

"I know." Daniel looked about. "Carla out?"

Sam nodded. "Visiting a new mother. She promised to take the older kids out and give the mom a rest."

"Don't you ever get tired of it? I mean, Carla's wonderful, but doesn't all that . . ."

"Do-gooding?" Sam suggested.

Daniel smiled wryly. "Doesn't it get to you after a while? Even the milk of human kindness has an expiration date."

Sam gave the expected laugh. He couldn't take offense at Daniel's flip words. Hadn't he thought the same thing when he'd first met Carla? "I thought so too. At one time."

"And now?"

"I know better."

Daniel flushed. "I didn't mean —"

"Jared calls her the preacher lady." Jared Walker, Sam's teenage buddy in the Reach-out program, hadn't known what to make of Carla either. He'd been afraid to trust her simple goodness. "Carla doesn't see her love that way."

"You've changed," Daniel said.

"For the better?"

"Definitely."

Sam's smile was full of tenderness. "I have Carla to thank for that."

"How do you know when it's right?" Daniel blurted out.

Sam didn't have to think about it. The answer came as easily as loving Carla did. "It's wanting to be with her all the time. It's knowing that you can't live without her and if you tried, you'd end up wishing you hadn't."

"You got it bad, buddy," Daniel said. Another time there would have been amusement, perhaps even a hint of derision in his voice. But now he felt only pleasure that his friend had found happiness. Pleasure mixed with envy.

Lately, he'd become aware of the holes in his life. Gaps he hadn't even been aware of. Maybe it was being around Sam and Carla and seeing the love they shared.

Maybe it was getting older. Maybe it was knowing his future was linked with that of the country and wanting a helpmeet to share it with him. Heck, maybe it was a lot of things.

Like a red-haired woman with golden eyes that always seemed to be laughing at him.

He'd been surprised at how right she'd felt in his arms. He'd expected her to feel good, and he hadn't been disappointed. What he hadn't expected was the *rightness,* the sense of having found something he'd spent all his life looking for.

"What're you going to do about her?" Sam asked.

"I'm going to marry her."

The words were out before he knew what he'd been about to say.

Sam didn't appear surprised. Well, Daniel reflected, his friend had always known what he was thinking before he became aware of it himself. Fifteen years hadn't changed that.

"Have you told Eve yet?" Sam asked. To his credit, there was only a touch of humor in his voice.

"No. I don't think she'll have me." The idea was hard to swallow, much less to voice aloud.

"I take it you have a plan to change her mind."

"I'm working on it," Daniel said. "I'm working on it."

He could be patient. He would give her the space she needed. A week, he promised himself. Surely, he could stay away for a week.

And then he would storm the barrier she had erected around her heart. He'd stage an old-fashioned siege. For the first time since Eve had given him his walking papers, Daniel smiled. His Scottish grandfather would have been proud of him.

Sam plucked a still-warm cookie from the plate Carla set in front of him. He finished it in two bites and washed it down with a glass of milk. "Daniel and I had a meeting this afternoon. He's got some ideas for funding more shelters that he wanted to go over with me."

Carla looked up from the oven, where she was removing another pan of cookies. "I've never known him to stay in town this long before."

"The Senate's in recess. He's decided to stay here and do a little grassroots campaigning for the next election."

"Maybe there's something else keeping

him here. Or someone."

Sam didn't bother asking her how she knew. Carla had an intuition about people that still amazed him.

She popped another cookie into his mouth.

"Eve told him to take a hike," he mumbled around the cookie. He swallowed. "I've never known Daniel to fail at anything. In college, he decided to play football. There were guys who were bigger and faster than he was, but he kept at it until he made the team."

Carla loosened the cookies from the pan and slid them onto a waiting plate. "Maybe he's met his match this time."

"Maybe. But my money's still on Daniel."

Sam looked at his wife and knew it could happen to anyone. At anytime. Hadn't he sworn he'd never marry? Carla had him tied up in knots within days of their first meeting. Heck, she even had his parents and him getting along these days. He knew how easily a woman — the right woman — could make a man forget everything, everything but the love.

"Daniel loves her."

"I think Eve loves him." She shook her head in answer to his unspoken question.

"She hasn't said anything. They love each other. It may not be enough."

Sam looked at his wife in surprise. He'd never heard Carla doubt the power of love, never believed she'd even questioned its strength. Now she was saying it might not be enough for two people he cared for very much.

"Eve hasn't talked much about her past, only enough to let me know she'll never go back to Washington."

"Never is a long time."

"She tried to make a home there, stayed for as long as she could. For her father's sake. When she couldn't take it any longer, she came here."

"What about Daniel? Don't his feelings count?"

"I think they count more than even he knows. She won't ask him to choose between her and his career."

Sam thought about the woman he'd come to know during the past months and knew Carla was right. Eve wouldn't ask Daniel to make a choice. He wondered what Daniel, given the chance, would choose.

Carla reached for him. Automatically, he closed his hand around hers. He'd do anything for this woman. He wondered if

Daniel felt the same for the woman he'd chosen as his own.

"Daniel's in love with her," he said again.

"What about Eve? Doesn't she have any say in the matter?"

"Did you?"

Her smile was answer in itself. Both knew they'd had no choice in loving the other. Both knew they'd have it no other way.

A whimper sounded over the nursery monitor. Carla started toward the stairs when Sam stopped her. "Let me get him."

He returned a few minutes later and handed Zach to her. "Here he is. Clean, dry, and hungry . . . not necessarily in that order."

Zach began rooting around. Carla settled in the rocking chair she'd placed in the kitchen and prepared to nurse him.

Sam felt tears sting his eyes. Watching her feed their son was one of the most beautiful experiences of his life. The intimacy of the act made it all the more precious.

She looked up, a tender smile touching her mouth. "It scares me sometimes how much I love you. How much I need you."

"However much you need me, I need

you even more." The words were nothing less than the truth. His life would be empty without Carla, and now Zach.

Sam found himself hoping Daniel could find the same happiness. He knew his friend was looking for something. He'd sensed the same searching for something in Daniel that he'd felt when he first met Carla.

He gathered her to him and found her lips. Thoughts about Eve and Daniel fled as he lost himself in the wonder that was Carla.

Chapter Six

Her feet hurt.

For the first time since she'd opened her shop, Eve looked forward to the end of the day. She curbed her impatience and pasted a pleasant smile on her face as she waited while a customer waffled between a set of place mats and a tablecloth.

When the place mats were decided upon, Eve boxed them, rang up the sale, and begged the lady to return soon. She prayed her words didn't sound as false as they felt.

Normally, she enjoyed the people who visited her shop. Wasn't that why she was in business? Because she liked people and wanted to be around them? So what was her problem now? She didn't have to look far for the answer to her impatience.

Daniel.

Despite her resolve to put him out of her mind, he'd persisted in invading her thoughts and infecting her dreams. Her customary determination had failed her.

She missed him. The admission left her shaken. When had she gotten to the point where she needed a man — not just any man, but a very special one — to make her day complete?

Well, she wasn't going to put up with it. She'd turned down an invitation earlier in the week for a party tonight. Her host had told her to drop by if she changed her mind. She headed to her room, pulled a dress from her closet, and started to get ready.

Daniel was not a creature of impulse. On the contrary, he relished discipline, method, and order. They were the hallmarks by which he lived his life.

Tonight, though, something prompted him to ignore the habits of a lifetime and go with impulse. He'd promised himself he'd give Eve a week. It had taken every ounce of self-control he could muster to stay away from her for six days, but he'd managed it.

Now he was going to forget his promise and go to her. If she were half as miserable as he was, he'd be satisfied. The honest corner of his brain called him a liar. He wouldn't be satisfied until she admitted her feelings for him.

He knew she wasn't indifferent. He knew she cared. He was pretty sure she was halfway in love with him. All she needed was to reach the same conclusion that he had: that they were meant for each other. No one appeared to answer the door when he jabbed at the bell. He settled on the porch swing and prepared to wait. He was still waiting when dusk had given way to night and stars studded the sky.

He consoled himself with the thought that waiting was the easy part. Convincing Eve to give him — to give them — a chance was going to be much harder. When a car door slammed, he started from the slight doze he'd fallen into. He looked up in time to see Eve climb out of a flashy sports car. A streetlight caught her in its glare, silhouetting her against the night.

Red.

Her dress was brilliantly, brazenly, boldly red.

She dispelled any remains of the old-fashioned notion that redheads shouldn't wear red. The dress glittered. It sparkled. It shimmered.

But no more so than the woman inside it.

Her hair, caught in a cascade of curls, rippled down her back in wave upon wave of copper and bronze, gold and mahogany, ginger and chestnut. Haloed beneath the streetlight, the colors shifted as she moved.

He stood, transfixed, and simply stared, forgetting that he'd been waiting by her front door for the better part of two hours, forgetting about his cold hands and colder feet, forgetting everything but the woman who had dominated his thoughts for the past weeks.

The breath whooshed from him as if he'd been felled by a blow. Each time he saw her, it was like seeing her for the first time all over again. Sure, he was struck by her beauty. What man wouldn't be? But it was more than that.

Looks aside, she radiated an energy, enthusiasm, and eagerness for life. Her very essence was one of joy. At times, he sensed an almost desperate desire in her to cram every moment full of living.

Was it because of what had happened to her mother? Of course it was, he answered his own question.

She waved good-bye to the carload of people who had dropped her off, her laughter floating back to him. She'd obviously been out partying. Jealousy tightened his lips as he saw her bend to kiss the driver good-bye. Less than a week since she'd dismissed him, and she was already seeing someone else.

She turned, saw him, and froze. When she started toward him, he couldn't wait.

He closed the remaining distance between them with three long strides and took her in his arms. "I couldn't stay away," he said at last.

Because she felt the same way, because she was so glad to see him, because she would have gone to him if he hadn't come to her, she walked into his arms. His strong arms. His gentle arms. His welcoming arms.

He rocked them both back and forth. She held on. For this moment, the past was gone, the future only a shadow. All that mattered was now.

He drew her hair to his nose. It smelled fresh and clean and slightly exotic, like one of the pots of potpourri she had scattered about her shop.

Eve pressed her face against his shoulder. He smelled of good, clean male. She clung tighter.

When they could bear to let each other go, she fumbled in her purse for her key. Her fingers were clumsy. Laughing, crying, she dumped the contents out on the porch. The keys gleamed under the porch light.

Daniel bent to help scoop things back into her purse, his fingers colliding with hers. Heat raced from his hand to her own.

She opened the door. Warmth greeted them.

Chilled hands chafed chilled hands. Hungry lips met hungry lips. Soft sighs echoed soft sighs.

He framed her face with his hands. "You're so beautiful."

It wasn't the first time he'd uttered those words to her. She hadn't believed him then. He doubted she believed him now. But he hadn't been able to keep the thought to himself, just as he couldn't keep from kissing her once more.

"Don't send me away again," he said. "I couldn't do it."

Her nod was an acknowledgment. And the beginning of a new start.

Eve believed the best way to teach was to show. When the middle school art teacher asked her to talk about her work, Eve did what she did best. She created.

She mixed and poured, measured and stirred, before she was satisfied with the results. She used natural ingredients — herbs, plants, even berries — to achieve the colors she wanted. Goldenrod for yellow, hickory nut for brown, indigo for blue.

Some students crowded around her, others hung back as Eve plopped a long swatch of material into a vat of dye and stirred it with a long-handled wooden spoon. "Don't be afraid of getting your hands in it." She demonstrated by plunging her arms into the vat, swishing the material back and forth. "When you've got the color you want, pull it out. If you want to do tone-on-tone, be ready with your next color."

"How come you don't just buy your clothes at the mall?" one girl asked. "Why go to all this work?"

Briefly Eve looked up from her task to glance at the girl. With her straight hair, T-shirt, and jeans, she was a clone of nearly every other girl in the class. "If I wanted to look like everyone else, I wouldn't." Titters of laughter told her that her remark had struck home.

She'd given the same demonstration to various art classes in elementary, middle, and high schools and had learned how to parry the questions thrown at her. The middle-schoolers proved to be the most difficult. Too old to appear to have fun with the dyes and too young to see the possibilities in creating their own clothes, they frequently resorted to putting down what she did as weird.

A few crowded around her to watch as she pulled the cloth from the vat. It was those whom Eve concentrated on.

"Wow," one girl breathed as Eve pulled a berry-colored cloth from the vat. A rosy pink streaked through the deeper color, giving it a multidimensional look. "I've never seen anything like it. Can I touch it?"

"Sure." Eve blotted the material between two old towels. "You can make your own colors, your own clothes."

"Did you make the dress you're wearing?"

"Mm-hmm. You like it?" She held out the folds of the full skirt dyed in various shades of blue, inviting the kids to touch it.

Hesitantly, the girl fingered the richly patterned dress. "It's beautiful. I'd give anything to be able to make something like that."

"How do you get the stripes and checks?" another girl asked, fingering a blanket of homespun wool.

Eve hid a smile. She had them now. Questions were a good sign. "I alternate natural-toned and dyed yarns. See?" She held up a piece of homespun, the original cream color striped with blue.

She dug a couple of cards out of her pocket and handed them to the girls. "Come on by my shop someday and I'll show you how to get started."

Daniel watched from the doorway. He'd tracked Eve down to the school. He needed to leave for Washington the next day and wanted to see her.

Looking at her now, he realized he'd stumbled across another facet to the woman he'd come to love. She handled the kids easily, neither talking down to them nor letting them intimidate her. She genuinely liked them, even the ones who hung back, making it clear she couldn't interest them. It showed in the way she took their questions seriously, the generous invitation to her workshop. She'd make a good mother, he reflected.

He knew the moment she'd spotted him. Color blossomed and rode high on her cheeks. She kept her attention focused on the teenagers, but her glance strayed to him occasionally. Was she glad to see him? The soft smile on her lips had him hoping she was.

When the art teacher took over, Eve made her way over to where Daniel waited.

Heedless of the teacher and class, he took her in his arms and kissed her lightly. Later, he promised himself, he'd kiss her properly. For now, he brushed his lips against hers and was gratified to see the widening of her eyes. Whatever her protestations to the contrary, the lady was not indifferent to him.

"Do you mind?" he asked. "I wanted to see you before I left."

"You're leaving?" The disappointment in her voice soothed away much of the pain of saying good-bye to her.

"I have to go to Washington for a few days. I'm running into some snags on a bill I'm trying to gather support for."

Daniel's words cut straight to her heart. Now that they were together, she begrudged anything that kept them apart. Including his job. Especially his job.

She nodded. "When?"

"Tonight." He brushed a kiss across her lips. He fitted a finger beneath her chin, tilting her head up so that their eyes met. "You'll think of me when I'm gone."

How could she argue with the obvious? Of course she'd think of him.

"But will you miss me?"

"You're head's big enough already."

"I'll take that as a yes. Have dinner with

me tonight." The invitation was an impulse. He had a dozen things to do before his flight. Right now, he couldn't remember a one of them. All that mattered was spending a few more hours with her.

Later, he couldn't have said where they'd gone, what they'd eaten, when they'd left to go home. All that he could think of was the woman at his side.

Inside her door, he caught her chin on the edge of his fist.

She kissed him fiercely. "Come back soon."

She missed him, darn it.

She thought of little — no, make that nothing else, but Daniel.

As she opened the door to the shop in the morning, she thought of him. When she rang up a sale, she thought of him again. And when she closed the store, she was still thinking of him.

The next five days stretched out before her, empty and bleak. There would be no surprise visits, no stolen kisses, no stimulating arguments.

The direction of her thoughts brought her up short. What was she thinking? Hadn't she claimed often enough that she didn't want those things, that her relationship with Daniel was one of simple friendship, that her heart was still whole?

She shoved those thoughts from her mind. What was she worried about, anyway? She could handle Daniel Cameron. Would handle him. After all, she hadn't known him long enough for him to matter.

After spending the better part of an hour convincing herself of that, she spread her hands.

She was in trouble.

Daniel had insinuated himself into her life as quietly as a baby's sigh. Only he wasn't a soft, cuddly infant. He was a large, demanding male who was fast becoming an integral part of her life. How had it happened? How had she *allowed* it to happen?

When she posed that question to Carla, who had arrived only minutes earlier, her friend hooted with laughter.

The two had been going through Eve's stock, looking for a gift for new parents in Carla's congregation. Carla turned her attention from the stack of baby blankets and focused it on Eve.

"You don't allow love to happen. It creeps up on you. It knocks you over the head. It shakes you until your teeth rattle. But it doesn't happen because you let it."

That drew a scowl from Eve. "I don't love him. I . . ." she searched for the proper word. "I care about him."

Carla gave her a look that said have it your own way, but Eve wasn't deceived. She knew Carla wasn't convinced.

With jerky determination, Eve dug through a pile of baby-sized blankets, shoving one after another to the side before she found the one she wanted. "What do you think of this?" she asked, holding up a pale blue shawl.

"Beautiful," Carla said. She fingered the finely spun cloth.

Eve placed the blanket in a tissue-lined box and quickly tied a bow made of the same yarn as the blanket around it.

Carla tucked it under her arm. "Thanks." She checked her watch. "I've got to run. Sam's watching Zach till I get back. Then he's off to a city council meeting."

Eve made a face. "Sounds boring."

"According to Sam, they usually are. But he's determined to get the funding approved for the new shelters."

Eve nodded. She knew how hard both Carla and Sam worked to improve the conditions of the homeless people of Saratoga.

When Carla left, Eve knew an acute sense of loneliness. Saturday afternoons were usually slow. Normally, Ron worked on the weekend, giving her time to experiment with new dyes or just take some time off. But he was taking his college boards today and didn't expect to be done until late in the afternoon. She'd assured him she'd manage without him.

Time dragged with a slowness that had her constantly checking the clock to see if it had stopped working. When she caught herself doing it for the fifth time in as many minutes, she knew it was time to do something about it.

It was Daniel's fault.

The man had forced himself into her life. That wasn't true, her conscience forced her to admit. She'd let him into her life.

He wasn't like any politician she'd ever met. Oh, she'd known honest politicians before. But it was more than that. Daniel radiated a kind of integrity that made others *want* to trust him. His dedication to the people went far beyond duty. It was borne out of genuine liking and caring.

He would someday be shooting for the oval office. It wasn't that he craved power; far from it. No, it was a need to make a difference that prompted him to seek the most powerful job in the world.

Stop it, she ordered herself. Think of

something else. Anything else.

It was pointless. Now that she'd let Daniel into her mind, she could think of nothing else but him. The way he looked with his hair mussed by a baby's hands. The way he tasted when his lips met hers. The way he made her feel. No doubt about it. He was firmly lodged in her mind.

Well, that didn't mean she was going to let him stay there. She shoved the image of his face away and concentrated on her work. The repetitive motion of operating the loom smoothed out the wrinkles of her thoughts. Nothing, though, could ease the loneliness that raged inside her heart.

The gifts started coming the next morning.

A basket of marbles. How had he known the brightly colored bits of glass would appeal to her? A dozen roses, a box of chocolates, she could have ignored. But the jewel-toned marbles drew her as nothing else could. Unable to help herself, she held one up to the light.

The man didn't play fair. Her breath came out in an annoyed gush that softened to a wistful sigh. No, he didn't play fair at all.

No other man had ever courted her with

such flair, such insight, such sensitivity, Eve decided the following day as she admired Daniel's latest gift — a basket of pansies. She opened the enclosed note. "They reminded me of you."

The card crumpled beneath her fingers. The man knew exactly what would please her. Why couldn't he be predictable, boring, and staid? Why did he have to be the one man who touched something deep inside her? She voiced the question aloud.

The purple-faced pansies seemed to nod in agreement.

"Delivery for you, Eve," Ron called out Friday afternoon.

Wiping her dye-stained hands on her bib apron, she left her work area for the shop.

"If you'll sign right here," the delivery boy said, and handed her a clipboard. The box bore an Australian postmark.

He hung around, clearly curious. To his and Ron's obvious disappointment, she took the box back to her workshop to open it in privacy.

As excited as a child at Christmas, she shook it. Impatiently, she slit the seams with a knife, opened the box, and dug among the packing papers. Her fingers encountered something soft. Eagerly, she pulled it free. A fleece. A tag identified it as Australian. Sheared and ready to card. Heedless of the lanolin that clung to it, she held it to her cheek.

The small card that accompanied it read, "Maybe someday you'll visit Australia with me." Daniel's name was scrawled at the bottom.

Oh, the man was good. He read her so easily, instinctively knowing what would please her.

She didn't like being that transparent. Didn't like it at all. Was she so obvious to everyone? Or was it just Daniel who could read her so easily? The latter caused her more than a little uneasiness. They'd known each other for less than a month, but she felt a connection between them that wasn't fixed by time or logic. Certainly not logic, she thought, her lips twisting in a wry smile.

Logic would have sent her running in the opposite direction from Daniel Cameron. Logic would suggest that she have her head examined for even thinking about going out with him. No, it darn sure wasn't logic that sparked the air with electricity whenever they were together.

Good manners dictated that she call and thank him for the gifts.

The telephone cut through the late-afternoon din of the office. Daniel shot to his feet, earning a startled look from his secretary, who'd been briefing him on an upcoming interview. "I've been expecting a call. I'll take it in your office."

Her eyebrows rose, but she was too well-trained to comment upon his odd behavior. He'd never bothered excluding her from his calls before. But, then, Eve had him doing a lot of things he'd never bothered with before.

He managed to reach the phone before the fourth ring. Anticipation was almost as good as reality. He pictured her, feet bare, legs tucked beneath one of those long, floating skirts of hers.

Daniel snugged the receiver next to his ear, feeling a grin already pulling at the corners of his mouth. "Cameron."

"It's Eve."

The feminine voice on the other end of the line was soft and, if he weren't mistaken, tinged with loneliness. He hoped it meant she missed him.

"The marbles, the pansies, the sheepskin . . . they're all beautiful. Thank you."

The reluctance in her voice warred with pleasure. The lady was weakening. He could feel it. "You're welcome."

"They're all very nice, but you don't have to —"

"I wanted to." There. Let her argue with that.

"The fleece . . . how did you know?"

He could hear the pique. "I took a guess. You like it?"

"I love it. It's the most wonderful present in the world."

He wondered what it would feel like to have her use the same words about him. A pleasurable warmth settled over his heart at the mere idea. Someday, perhaps, he'd know.

He could hear her shifting the receiver against her ear, guessing that she was settling on the tall stool in her workroom. Her hair would be pulled on top of her head in a knot of curls, a few escaping to tumble down her cheeks and neck. For a moment, he indulged in a fantasy of picturing himself pulling the pins from her hair and freeing the remaining curls.

"Daniel?"

"Hmmm?"

"I meant what I said. No one has ever given me such beautiful things."

He was wearing her down, Daniel decided. What other woman would think a hunk of sheepskin was beautiful? But, then, he was learning that Eve wasn't like any other woman.

"I miss you." He waited. Hoping.

"I . . . I miss you too."

His heart leapt. The admission had cost her, he knew. She was still resisting what was happening between them. But he'd scored a victory. A small one, but a victory nonetheless.

"See me when I get back?" He didn't give her a chance to answer. "I get in tomorrow night. Around eight." With that, he hung up.

The dial tone ringing in her ear, she replaced the receiver, fighting the desire to smile and an equally strong one to throw something.

Who did he think he was, assuming that she wanted to see him, that she would see him, just because he crooked his finger? Well, he might just find her out when he came calling. He might just find she had other plans. He might just . . .

Who was she trying to kid? She missed him more than she thought possible.

Eve finished closing the shop, humming a Broadway song. She might have wished Daniel weren't quite so charming. Or that she didn't enjoy herself quite so much when she was with him.

She might have wished for all of those things. But she didn't. She was happy. And it was due to Daniel.

No, that wasn't right. It was due to how she felt when she was with him. He made her laugh. At herself. At him. At life in general. What greater gift was there?

She put aside the niggling doubts as to where they were heading. For now she was content. She spent the better part of the day in the kitchen. Cooking.

The word normally had her cringing. Cooking was one of the few things she'd tried that she hadn't excelled in. Face it, she ordered herself silently, she hadn't even passed the junior high omelette test.

But, for Daniel, she was determined to try.

By a quarter to eight, she was ready to consign all cookbook authors to a special place in purgatory. Her roast was overdone, her potatoes still raw, and her vegetables limp. The only thing she hadn't managed to ruin was dessert, and only because she'd picked it up from a bakery.

Daniel arrived a few minutes later, took in the shambles of her kitchen, and promptly picked up the phone. That completed, he took her in his arms and kissed her.

She responded with equal fervor.

"You did miss me," he said in satisfaction, with a smile that was every bit as devastating as his kiss.

She guarded herself against that smile he used to such advantage. Any man who smiled like that needed extra care in handling.

"I brought you something." He handed her a small, rectangular package.

Eagerly, she ripped away the brown wrapping paper to uncover a first edition of a Nancy Drew story, *The Mystery of the Old Clock*. No hearts and flowers from Daniel Cameron, but a book she'd treasured as a child. How had he known?

She opened the book, turning the pages reverently, unable to stifle a gasp of pleasure. "Thank you."

"You're welcome. Now, let's get this place cleaned up. It looks like a tornado just whirled through."

She made a face and threw a dishrag at him. Within a half hour, the kitchen was restored to order. Minutes later, a delivery boy showed up.

Daniel paid him, added a tip, and kissed Eve.

"What was that for?" she asked.

"For not being perfect. If you'd been perfect in the kitchen like you are everywhere else, I'd start to worry I wasn't good enough for you."

It was her turn to kiss him now. And she did. What had started as a disaster had turned into fun. All because of Daniel.

"What did you want to do when you were a kid?" he asked as he pulled out cartons of Cantonese chicken, wonton soup, and egg rolls.

She bit into an egg roll. "The usual. A ballerina."

"Why didn't you go for it?"

"I did. I took lessons from the time I was six until I was sixteen."

"What happened?"

"This. I grew up. Five feet and ten inches up. When was the last time you saw a ballerina this tall?"

"Did you mind giving up your dream?" he asked, setting the cartons on the table.

"A little." She shrugged. "Then I found a new one. What about you?"

"When I was six, I wanted to be an explorer. You know, like Columbus. Or Balboa. Finding new lands, claiming them for my country. By the time I was eight, I decided to be an astronaut."

Eve tried to picture Daniel as an eight-year-old boy. He had probably been a tad serious, with questioning eyes and a smile that peeked out at unexpected moments. She liked the image.

She could also picture the children he'd have. Small boys with hair the color of rich chocolate, and solemn eyes. He'd be a good father.

Image after image crowded her mind, and she shook her head to dispel them. Daniel as a father wasn't a picture she particularly wanted to dwell on. Especially when the children weren't likely to be hers.

Chapter Seven

An invitation for the two of them to have dinner with Sam and Carla Sunday night was a pleasant change from the week he'd spent in Washington. There, he felt that he was constantly on. On display. On demand. *On*.

Relaxing with friends was a refreshing contrast. The home-cooked meal, easy conversation, and lack of interruptions eased away much of the tension of the last week.

Following dinner, they relaxed in the front room. Watching Carla cuddle Zach aroused unexpected feelings within Daniel. "Can I hold him?" he asked.

Carla looked surprised, then smiled. "Sure." She settled Zach into his arms.

Automatically, Daniel tightened his hold on the baby, finding he liked the sensation. He skimmed a finger down Zach's cheek. Soft. Involuntarily, he sought Eve's eyes, needing to share the moment with her. The smile that touched her lips had a matching one tugging at his own.

Eve bent over to drop a kiss on Zach's cheek, her hair falling across her face. He grabbed a fistful and held fast.

Without stopping to think, Daniel untangled the silky strands from the tiny fingers, his hand colliding with Eve's. Heat arched from skin to skin. "Hey, fellow, that's no way to treat a lady. Besides, this one's spoken for."

His careless words had Carla and Sam exchanging glances and Eve flushing, whether with embarrassment or anger, he wasn't sure. Probably the latter, he decided. She hadn't given him the right to use those words.

Zach let out a lusty wail that had everyone scrambling to pacify him and distracting them, Daniel noted with relief, from his ill-chosen words.

Eve dangled a rattle in front of Zach. "See," she crooned. "You like that, don't you?"

The baby's abrupt switch from crying to gurgling had the four adults chuckling.

"He's already learned how to get what he wants," Sam said, drawing another round of chuckles.

A suspicious warmth spread across Daniel's chest, causing him to grimace. "I think Zach's due for a diaper change," he said, holding the baby away from him.

Carla reached for her son.

"Let me," Eve volunteered and, heedless of his wet condition, cuddled Zach to her.

Daniel couldn't help it. His gaze followed her until she'd disappeared down the hallway.

He managed to ignore the significant looks exchanged by Carla and Sam and hoped they kept whatever it was they were thinking to themselves. The last thing he needed was advice to the lovelorn, even if it was from good friends.

"The boy's already got an eye for the ladies," Sam said.

Daniel could only admire his godson's taste.

Later, as he saw Eve home, he thought of the evening they'd shared at their friends' home. He wanted that for himself, he realized. A home and all that went with it — a wife, children, wet diapers and all. As if to punctuate his thoughts, his shirt clung damply to him, and he shifted uncomfortably.

"How'd you like being christened?"

"Christened?" He chuckled as her meaning became clear. "I'll survive."

"Some men wouldn't take it so well. You handled it like a pro."

The compliment pleased him. He'd received honorary degrees from universities, been awarded plaques for his work with the homeless, but none meant as much as Eve's words.

He had it bad, he thought. The woman had but to give him the smallest bit of praise, and he was lapping it up like a starved kitten licking out a tuna fish can.

It didn't bother him. One more sign that he was well and truly hooked. "Have you ever thought of opening up another shop? Somewhere else?"

Absently, she stacked magazines into piles. "Not really. Why?"

"I was just wondering if you could be happy living somewhere else."

Leave Saratoga?

She liked the town — the wide streets and family-owned stores that kept country hours, the quiet neighborhoods tucked in between the business districts. People knew your business and didn't mind telling you how to mind it if you strayed from what they considered the straight and narrow.

Saratoga wasn't without its problems.

She knew enough to understand that even small towns weren't immune to the troubles that plagued today's world. Still, it had become home. Home, she'd learned, wasn't a matter of birthplace but of the heart.

Aware that Daniel was waiting for her answer, she tried a smile. "I hadn't really thought about it."

"Maybe someday you will." He left it at that, and she was grateful.

She knew he was coming close to asking for something she wasn't ready to give, didn't know if she'd ever be able to give.

Daniel had endured the black-tie affair with local party leaders for as long as he could. After nearly a week away from Eve, he had no desire to spend even a single night making political small talk.

When the last course was over, he nudged Eve.

"Let's get out of here," he whispered.

"Can we?"

The longing in her voice had him grinning. "You bet." He took her elbow and guided her through the clusters of people. "How does pizza sound?" he asked, once they were in the car.

"Great."

"Do you think anyone's going to notice you're in a tuxedo?" she asked as they walked into the pizzeria.

He looked down at his tux. He might escape with little attention, but not Eve. She was a knockout in a long blue dress that hugged every one of her five feet and ten inches.

"No one's going to pay any attention to me," he said.

The shrill of whistles from a group of teenage boys huddled in a corner booth made his point. His hand tightened on her waist. She handled the situation with a smile toward the boys that had them blushing and stammering apologies, which she waved off.

She had no idea how special she was. Most women of his acquaintance would have made a scene, but not Eve. She treated the boys with a manner that put them all at ease and defused what could have been a tense situation.

A teenage waitress seated them at a booth and handed them menus. "Be back in a minute," she said, and left to flirt with the boys.

"What looks good?" Daniel asked, scanning the menu.

"Extra cheese, ham, pepperoni, green

peppers, mushrooms, and onion," Eve said promptly. "And a side order of garlic bread and a salad."

Daniel raised a brow. "If I'd realized you were going to order the whole menu, I'd have brought along more money."

She ignored that. "And a couple of pitchers of root beer."

He repeated the order to the waitress.

One of the boys fed quarters into the jukebox. Music heated up the room. Eve tapped her fingers in time to the beat. Daniel leaned across the table so that she could hear him.

"You like this kind of thing?" he asked.

"Yeah. Does that surprise you?"

A quick grin slid across his lips. "I'm learning not to be surprised when it comes to you."

"I think I've been complimented." She cocked her head to one side. "Or insulted."

"The first. Definitely the first."

They sat back to listen to the music. "Good thing we weren't planning on talking," Daniel shouted over the rap beat.

Her eyes lit with amusement. She'd bet her favorite loom that he hadn't spent an evening like this in a long time. If ever. He was a good sport about it, though. How many men did she know who would be content to eat pizza at a hangout frequented by local teenagers?

Their food arrived, two deluxe pizzas with the requested side orders. Eve tucked a paper napkin under the neckline of her dress and prepared to enjoy herself.

Daniel laid his napkin across his lap and reached for a piece.

Eve bit into the pizza. “Mmmmm.”

He dabbed at her chin with his napkin. “Cheese,” he said solemnly.

“It’s a disgrace,” she said between bites. “Two adults sneaking out of a party just so they can go for pizza.”

“Want to go back?” he asked.

She gave him a black look. “You try taking me back, and I’ll be forced to hurt you.”

“That’s what I thought.” He handed her another piece.

Rock music, pizza, and paper napkins hardly equaled a romantic evening. But the most important ingredients were there — a man and a woman in love.

It occurred to her that this was a moment that would linger in her memory, one she would cherish. The two of them eating pizza, licking their fingers, and squabbling over the last piece like children.

It wasn’t the big moments that made up

a life, she reflected, but the small ones. That's what she wanted — a string of small memories that added up to a lifetime.

The evening set the tone for the days that followed. Stolen moments in the middle of the day, a meal shared at the day's end, and kisses so sweet that they took her breath away.

Whatever her life had been before, Daniel had changed it simply by stepping into it. She doubted she'd ever be able to look at marbles or pansies in quite the same way again. And it was certain she'd never eat pizza again without thinking of him.

Her lips twitched into a small smile as she remembered how they'd snuck away from dinner like naughty children to eat pizza and steal an evening alone.

Through it all, Eve knew she was falling more and more in love with Daniel. She had no one to blame but herself. She'd gone into it with her eyes open, her heart, she thought, safeguarded against the perils of love.

She had no time to worry over it now. The shop was open, and she had a customer waiting.

"I want something for my niece's daughter's wedding," Mrs. Miller said.

Eve felt her spirits lift at the mention of a wedding. Helping customers choose something special for someone they loved was one of the nicest things about owning a shop. Besides, she could always count on Mrs. Miller for the freshest gossip, mixed with a dash of compassion.

She'd met Mrs. Miller through Carla. The older woman was the biggest gossip in the church and, possibly, the whole town. She also had a heart to match.

"What did you have in mind?"

"I was thinking about place mats. Maybe a tablecloth. Something flowered."

Eve didn't bother pointing out that she didn't do flowers. Instead, she moved to where she kept the linens and gestured to a set of woven place mats.

Mrs. Miller fingered the mats, but her gaze was trained on Eve. "I hear you've been seeing our handsome senator."

Saratoga's grapevine was alive and well, Eve thought. She didn't mind. Not when she knew the curiosity was prompted by caring. "You hear right."

Mrs. Miller gave her an arch look, her baby-blue eyes brightening at the confirmation of the gossip. "The Camerons go way back. I recollect Estelle — Daniel's grandmother. She was a Van Buren back then. She had more beaux than a body could count. 'Course, I had my share too." Pointedly, she paused.

Eve gave the expected nod and waited.

"Estelle could've had any boy she wanted, but she had her heart set on Henry Cameron. Got him too. They had two boys. First one died in the war. Second one sowed his share of wild oats and then some. Settled down after he got himself married to one of the Sinclair girls and had his sons. Daniel favors him. Of course, the Camerons have always been in public service. When a family's got as much money as they do, what else is there to do?"

Mrs. Miller stopped to catch her breath, giving Eve time to digest what she'd learned.

The tradition of service was one Daniel had been born to. Hadn't she already known how deep his commitment to the country ran? Unlike many politicians, he did it out of genuine caring rather than a lust for power.

"He's considered quite a catch," the older woman said, her speculative eyes still resting on Eve.

"Is he?"

Mrs. Miller's smile widened. "You're a pretty girl. And a nice one." Her double chins wagged as she chuckled. "You could do worse than a handsome senator. They say he'll go all the way." She looked about and then lowered her voice. "The White House."

Eve managed a smile. "They could be right."

Clearly disappointed at not receiving more of a response, Mrs. Miller picked out a set of place mats. "I do wish you had something with flowers, but this pretty design is eye-catching enough."

That pretty design was the result of hours spent perfecting the right dyes, but Eve wasn't offended. She understood Mrs. Miller and appreciated the older woman's business. Mrs. Miller had been one of the first to patronize Eve's shop. She'd encouraged her friends to shop there as well. As a result, her shop was extremely popular with the blue-haired ladies.

With the transaction completed, Mrs. Miller said a reluctant good-bye. Eve barely kept her laughter in check at the older woman's frustration with Eve's failure to provide her with additional gossip.

When the door closed, she gave in to the chuckle stuck in her throat. Her amusement faded as she acknowledged what she'd only recently admitted to herself.

Love. She'd shied away from the word until now.

If she hadn't been so caught up in convincing herself that all she felt for him was friendship, she'd have recognized the symptoms before now. The ease she felt when she was with Daniel, the trust that came from knowing she could say anything and he would understand, the pain she experienced when they were apart, all were part of love.

She could no longer deny her feelings for him. Hiding from the truth was cowardly. Not to mention stupid. Better to face it. She was in love with Daniel Cameron, and she knew he returned that love. She also knew he was close to asking her to share his destiny.

Daniel had enjoyed women in the past. Their softness and compassion, their wit and humor, all the ways that they differed from men. But there'd never been a woman who was specifically important, as Eve had become, never been a woman who had touched his heart in the same way.

He was in love with her. Daniel had always prided himself on being logical. The logical step from love was marriage. He tasted the word upon his lips, hearing its rightness.

He'd always expected to marry. Someday. The simple fact was the public expected its leaders to be married. Still, he'd never take such a step if he wasn't in love.

Now, he was.

Gloriously, wonderfully, irrevocably in love.

A frown chased away his smile as he thought about Eve's reaction. She'd need time to adjust to the idea of marriage. He was prepared for that. Law was an exacting science, one requiring infinite patience and tenacity. Fortunately, he had plenty of both.

The biggest surprise was that he hadn't needed to adjust to the idea. It had simply appeared, full-blown, in his mind. Or maybe, he decided, in his heart. His lips curved into a faint smile. Lately, his heart had taken charge. And he'd never been happier.

That evening, he talked about Washington, painting it in such glowing colors that even Eve, who'd been born and raised there, saw it with fresh excitement.

But that didn't mean she wanted to live there. Her home was here. How did she explain that Saratoga was the home of her heart, if not of her birth?

"I need . . ." she began.

"What?"

"To belong somewhere." She searched for the words to explain her feelings. "The continuity of being a part of something bigger than myself, the connection of community."

"And you've found that here . . . in Saratoga?"

She knew Saratoga wasn't without problems. It had its share of crime and homelessness, but it still had a small-town flavor that gave her the sense of community she longed for. She'd made a place for herself here. Her art and her friends had seen to that.

"Even though I wasn't born here, I feel a connection." The happiest moments of her childhood had been spent here. In her grandmother's house. "Roots go deep, even secondhand ones."

He understood. That warmed her. It also gave her courage to say what she needed to say. "This is my home. This is where I belong."

"No problem. I like Saratoga. I always have."

"But your work . . ."

"We can stay here when Congress isn't

in session. When it is, we'll travel back and forth. Lots of people do it."

She wanted to scream. *But I'm not lots of people*. But she kept silent.

"Washington's a beautiful city," he repeated, as if the place itself was what stood between them.

Perhaps, she thought, they focused on that because it was easier, safer, than the real problem. His job.

Her nod was perfunctory. She'd tried making it in Washington. For her father's sake, she'd tried. With his teaching post at Georgetown University, he belonged there. But he'd understood when she admitted that she was slowly dying there and had encouraged her to move to the one place she'd felt truly at home — Saratoga.

Daniel's hands closed gently upon her shoulders. "You know how I feel, Eve. What I want."

She did know.

At her continued silence, he sighed. "I'd like to spend the rest of the afternoon proving just how much I love you." He kissed the curve of her neck. "But I've got a stack of papers to go through before my trip."

His job again. He'd been away from the center of his work for too many weeks. A man in Daniel's position would always have work. He couldn't close shop if he wanted to take a few hours off. Or hire someone else to take over. No, being a United States senator demanded everything he had to give.

Technically, this trip was for social reasons — an invitation to a party. The party, to be held at the vice president's house, was important beyond the social aspect, though. Daniel had told her enough in the last few weeks for her to understand that he needed the support of several key members of the House and the Senate in order to get his new bill passed.

He snapped his fingers. "Come with me."

"To Washington?"

"To Washington."

"Just like that?"

"Just like that." He took her hand. "Just for the weekend. We'll fly back the next evening. My mother keeps an apartment in Georgetown. You can stay there."

As a child, she'd been accustomed to the pick-up-and-leave-at-a-moment's-notice type of life. Public life demanded that its servants be able to go where and when the job demanded.

"If I promise to have you back by midnight Sunday, will you say yes?"

She had a wild desire to laugh. Would the plane turn into a pumpkin if he failed to make good on his promise? And what about her? What would happen to her? Cinderella, she wasn't. And she wasn't looking for the handsome prince to rescue her.

"One of us has to be sensible," she said, sounding hopelessly prim.

"Why?"

The question coming from the oh-so-proper Senator Cameron surprised a laugh from her. "I don't know why. I just know one of us has to be."

"I'll tell you what. You be sensible. I'll be . . ." He whispered in her ear.

Her eyes widened. "Senator, shame on you."

"You'll come."

The banter was gone from his voice. All that remained was a quiet request. One she didn't think she could deny.

"Okay."

He skimmed his lips along her jaw. "You won't be sorry. I promise."

She was afraid she was already sorry. Not for agreeing to accompany him to Washington, but because she'd gone and done what she'd promised herself she would never do: she'd fallen in love with him.

In the next two days, she packed, worried, cleaned up her workroom, worried, dusted every inch of her shop, and worried some more. Not about the trip. But about what Daniel expected from her following the trip.

Daniel stopped by the night before they were due to leave. "There's something I wanted . . . needed . . . to say." He swallowed. Hard. "I think you know what I want, what I'm asking." He waited.

Her nod, barely there, acknowledged her understanding.

"I want to spend the rest of my life with you. I'm asking you to marry me, Eve."

Her hands, normally so graceful, so sure in their movements, fluttered nervously. "I can't —"

He forestalled what he feared was a refusal. "You don't have to give me your answer now. Wait until we get back."

The relief in her eyes told him he'd done the right thing by not pressuring her for an answer now. Time was on his side. He intended using every minute, every moment, to convince her that they belonged together.

His hopes raised another notch when she

took his hand and laid it against her cheek. "You're good to me."

He wanted to tell her that he was good *for* her, that they were good for each other. Instead, he skimmed his fingers along her jaw and tried to say with his touch what he couldn't put into words.

There was one thing he could say, though. One thing that she couldn't challenge, couldn't deny. "I love you."

"I know."

Why couldn't he take comfort in those two words? Was that regret he heard? He pushed his fears aside and worked up a stiff smile. "I'll pick you up at eight."

Eve watched as he shook his head, as though he didn't like the direction his thoughts had taken.

"I'll be ready," she promised.

The sigh of relief that whispered from her when Daniel left shamed her. Heaven help her, she wasn't ready. She wasn't sure she would ever be ready. Why couldn't they continue on as they had? Why did he have to complicate everything with a proposal?

Yet how could he do anything else? Daniel was an honorable man, a courageous one. He deserved a woman who was equally honorable, equally courageous. She was neither. She wanted him, but on her own terms. She wasn't selfless enough to share him with the entire country or brave enough to risk him to an assassin's bullet.

She feared she couldn't give him what she knew he wanted, but she could give them this weekend together.

Chapter Eight

Washington. The nation's capital. *Home*. An ache in her chest swelled so that she could scarcely breathe; her hands trembled within her gloves. A piercing sweetness went through her. A lifetime ago, she'd loved this city.

She'd left Washington over ten years ago, shortly after she'd graduated from high school. She'd tried sticking it out, for her father's sake. When she found that she couldn't, she'd moved to Saratoga and lived with her grandmother while she went to college. When her grandmother died five years ago, Eve had inherited the house, a small trust fund, and a love for her adopted hometown.

A late snowstorm had reduced Washington traffic to a crawl. Eve didn't mind. The city normally moved at a frantic pace. In everything. Cold and ice hadn't shut the city down, but they had slowed it down.

She was grateful for the opportunity to catch her breath.

Washington glistened under its layer of new snow, giving the city a fairy-tale appearance. On the streets, reality intruded, though, as exhaust fumes turned the pristine white a muddy gray. Much like the character of the city, she thought. Glittering on the outside, soiled beneath the surface.

She recognized her attitude for what it was. Prejudice, laced with pain. She had never been able to view the city objectively. As a child, she'd seen only the gleam of marble monuments and the twinkle of the ladies' jewels.

That picture had died along with her mother.

She yanked her thoughts back to the present. She'd promised herself, more importantly, she'd promised Daniel, this weekend. A fantasy in a city that had once been likened to Camelot. But Camelot had crumbled.

She knew the importance of dressing for Washington parties, where appearances counted more than substance. Her strategy was simple: surprise. Her jewel-toned flowing pants and floor-length tunic were hardly Washington-party fare. Shot with gold threads, they glimmered with every movement. Conventional they were not. For a moment, she wondered if her attire might embarrass Daniel.

The look in his eyes when he arrived to pick her up bolstered her confidence.

"How do you do it?" he asked, spinning her around.

"Do what?"

"Manage to be more beautiful each time I see you."

"Save your flattery for the party, Senator," she said, wanting to dispel the quivery sensation that had settled in the pit of her stomach at his words.

"The truth's not flattery." He dropped her evening shawl over her shoulders, his touch doing nothing to disperse the butterflies that flitted around her heart.

The party was pure Washington. Designer dresses and safety deposit jewels. Champagne and canapés. Power handshakes and plastic smiles.

She accepted them for what they were. More than any city on earth, with the exception of Hollywood, Washington was built upon illusion. It was an illusion all worked hard to maintain. If that illusion were allowed to crumble, the whole house of cards might collapse.

Conversation buzzed, competing with the music. Eve circulated with the ease that came from growing up on the political circuit. She held her own when she disagreed with a Supreme Court justice who had singled her out to be the recipient of his latest views and barely managed to extricate herself when the tirade threatened to continue for another hour.

When Daniel appeared at her side, she managed a smile. Not for anything would she ruin this evening for him.

"I'm fine," she said when he showed a tendency to hover. "Go do your thing."

"What about you?"

"I'm going to sample the food." To prove her words, she plucked a caviar-laden cracker from a tray.

When Daniel hesitated, she gave him a little push. "Go. I'll yell if I need rescuing."

"What if I need rescuing?"

She reached up to brush a kiss across his cheek. "I'll be there."

Filling her plate with an assortment of fancy finger foods, she settled back to indulge in her favorite pastime at such functions: people-watching. The guest list was as impressive as the setting. An ambassador and a visiting dignitary. A Supreme Court justice and a pro football player. A prince from a Mideast country and America's own kind of royalty — a movie star.

But the real work was taking place in the corners, where deals were made.

She was seasoned enough in the rituals of political socializing to recognize the favor-trading and deal-making as necessary. But that didn't mean she had to like them.

She watched Daniel. He moved with an easy assurance. He filled her with pride, not just for who he was, but for what he was: a man devoted to making a difference.

When word got around that she was Daniel's date, she attracted more attention than she wanted.

The constant questions, the assumption that their relationship was fodder for public consumption, ate away at her. She understood that when one entered public life, one gave away any private life. What she resented was that her life was also considered fair game.

Daniel slipped up behind her, placing his hands on her waist and nuzzling her ear. Shimmers of pleasure danced down her spine at his touch. When a photographer aimed his camera at them, she felt her enjoyment slide away.

"Smile."

The order had her lips turned up in an

unnatural curve that felt stiff and stilted. Daniel's hand tightened around hers. She squeezed back, grateful for the contact.

"Do you want to get out of here?" he asked.

More than she wanted her next breath, but she didn't tell him that. The party was important to Daniel. Therefore, it was important to her.

"When you're finished," she said.

The grateful look he gave her warmed her as she watched him walk away.

This was Daniel's world, she reminded herself. She'd been deluding herself if she believed the weeks in Saratoga could continue indefinitely.

Washington was his home. And, she feared, his destiny.

He was a heartbreak waiting to happen. Somehow, he'd pushed and finagled his way into her life. She still didn't quite know how it had happened. He had forced his way into her life, and it was hard — no, make that impossible — to picture a day going by without seeing him, without the sight of him sending her heart into a full-fledged gallop. With each day, it became harder and harder to remember why she couldn't have a future with him.

Alone, she could summon the reasons

with no problem. When he was with her, though, her good sense fled and all that remained was a soul-deep need to be with him. What would happen when she lost even that bit of sanity?

The thought was enough to leave her trembling. Daniel threatened everything she'd striven for over the last ten years.

Images of them laughing, working, and traveling together tumbled through her mind. Love danced in front of her, close enough for her to touch.

Daniel could be anything he chose. She knew his desire to serve ran deep. There were countless opportunities for him to make a difference in the country. It didn't have to be within the arena of politics.

She shook her head, dispelling the notion.

This particular fantasy had no basis in reality. Even if he were willing to abandon his profession — it was more than that, his calling — she couldn't allow it. She loved him too much to ask him to give up what he was so obviously born to do.

She opened her eyes and looked again at Daniel. He was deep in conversation with a portly gentleman who gestured in her direction. Probably discussing her suitability, she thought sourly.

Ashamed of her thoughts, she ducked her head. Daniel wasn't like that. He would never ask her to be anything other than what she was. She could do no less for him.

Daniel wasn't surprised when Senator Howard Canfield, a staple on the Washington scene, cornered him. "I've been asked to approach you." Daniel waited for Canfield to continue. "It's early days yet, but not so early we can let the grass grow under our feet." Canfield laughed at his own joke.

"What do you want, Senator?"

The older man cleared his throat. "No beating around the bush for you, is there, Cameron? Some of the party leaders have their eye on you for the top office."

Daniel had been expecting it. Still, hearing it put into words jolted him. "I've been thinking along those lines myself," he said cautiously.

"Then you know we've got a long haul in front of us. We'll have a fight on our hands." Canfield rubbed his hands together with the relish of a seasoned campaigner. "Not that you can't handle it." He coughed. "There's one thing. The people like their leaders happily married."

He followed Daniel's gaze to where Eve

occupied the center of a group. In a room where most of the women appeared clones of each other, she sparkled with life and energy and color.

"She's a bright girl. I knew her family, of course. She dropped out of Washington years ago. Lacks polish, but that can be acquired."

Daniel's eyes narrowed. This was exactly what Eve had tried to tell him, and he'd brushed it aside. Now he realized he'd been foolish in dismissing her concerns. "Eve's not required to be anything except what she is."

"Well . . . of course, *I* like the girl. But there are others who aren't as broad-minded."

"Tell the *others* —" Daniel stressed the word "— that Eve's not part of the package."

"Don't be naive," Canfield snapped. "Any man aiming for the top rung is fair game. And that includes his family." With that, he patted Daniel's shoulder and took himself off.

Daniel struggled with his anger. Not at the other senator — the man had only been speaking the truth — but at himself. He'd known, of course, what public life entailed. But he'd blinded himself to it. Because he wanted both. He wanted a shot at the presidency. Not for the power involved. Never that. Only a fool craved that kind of power. No, he wanted to help shape the future of the country he loved.

He also wanted Eve.

He threaded his way through the crowd and found her. Slipping his arm around her waist, he felt the tension within her coil tighter and tighter. Laughter, conversation, and music swirled around them, but the pain in her eyes made a mockery of the party atmosphere. She looked up. Her lips curved brightly, but the smile didn't move to her eyes.

He wondered if she knew how easily she fit into the political world, despite her professed disdain of it. She could hold her own in any setting, he realized, but she sparkled here. If only she could put aside her fears, she might find the excitement, the energy that he always felt while in Washington.

Granted, the parties and socializing weren't his favorite part. He recognized them for what they were: camouflage for the real business of power-brokering. Accusations that he had a white-hat syndrome had been tossed his way over the years. He wasn't ashamed of the fact that he wanted to make a difference. That he chose to do it from the public arena rather than from the private sector had been a carefully made choice.

Family tradition had played a part. He wouldn't deny it. But not even the practice of generations could persuade him to do what he didn't truly want to. And he wanted this.

But he wanted, no, he *needed* Eve by his side. Without her, none of it mattered. He loved her in a way he'd never loved another woman. She touched something deep within his soul. She filled places he hadn't known were empty, answered questions he hadn't thought to ask. He couldn't picture a future without her.

He'd find a way to lay her fears about his profession to rest. His lips flattened in determination. The alternative wasn't an option.

He'd promised Eve that he'd wait until their return from Washington to ask her to marry him again. Nearly a week had passed, and he'd yet to fulfill his promise. He'd tried, but she'd always managed to sidetrack him from his intention. She had a movie she wanted to see, an art show to attend, a new idea for a design she had to get down on paper.

Well, no more. It was time to confront it head-on.

He had to stop letting his fear dictate his actions. He could worry about losing Eve forever, but worry never accomplished anything. It never had.

He found her in her workroom. The carefully chosen words he'd planned to say vanished as he took in the tear-shiny brightness of her eyes.

He didn't know what had put the tears there, but he had a good idea that it had to do with him. The knowledge filled him with guilt. And hope. If she were troubled enough about him — about them — to cry, then maybe it meant she loved him and realized what he had weeks ago: they belonged together.

Eve didn't know she was vulnerable. She was too busy trying to be independent and tough. He admired both qualities. That didn't mean he couldn't appreciate the softer side he knew she kept hidden inside. It was up to him to show her that she could be both without losing any of herself.

He took her in his arms. Seconds bled into minutes, and still he held her. He put her from him just long enough to wipe away the tears with the pads of his thumbs.

"Why the tears?" he asked.

She shook her head. "No reason."

He didn't buy that. Not for a minute. Eve wasn't a woman to cry for no reason, but he let it pass. For now.

"You know why I'm here."

"You want an answer."

He nodded. "I love you. You love me. It's that simple."

Her laugh was strained. "I wish it were. Only you and me. But it's not."

He wanted to argue with that, but she'd spoken only the truth. His next words confirmed it. "I should tell you, I've been approached by some members of the party to run for president. It won't be for another eight years, maybe more, but the wheels are already in motion. I need you by my side, Eve."

The time had come. Daniel had given her the promised time and then some. She'd waited, hoping . . . for what, she didn't know. Some kind of divine intervention, she supposed. To change the past? To give her courage? To turn Daniel into a baker, a shoemaker, a candlestick maker? Anything but what he was — a politician destined to reach the top rung.

She turned away, needing to occupy her hands. Normally her fingers eased the threads through the loom with ease, but not tonight. They fumbled, not pulling the thread tight enough and then stretching it too taut. It snapped. And so did her temper. She uttered something she'd never said before.

Large hands settled on her shoulders, turning her around. "Don't."

"I have to get this finished. It's a special order and I haven't even started." She was babbling. What's more, she'd lied. Her client had specifically said there was no hurry.

"This concerns both of us. I want to know what you think."

"Of course, you should run when the time comes. There's no one better, no one who cares as much."

That's what it came down to. Caring.

Politicians spouted phrases like family values, morality, ethics, all the time. But not Daniel. Perhaps because he wasn't a politician. He was a statesman. He didn't give lip service to the buzz words; he lived them. He'd work to make things better, not just for the privileged class of which he was a member, but for all the citizens.

Good grief. She was starting to sound like some kind of political speech writer.

"This is what you were born for." She

managed to say the words calmly enough, even as they ripped the heart from her. Not because she didn't believe them. But because she did.

"I need you by my side, Eve. I can't do it on my own." He took her hand and brought it to his lips. "Marry me."

Her laugh sounded almost genuine. Almost. "I didn't know you were also a comedian."

A muscle twitched in his neck. "I was never more serious in my life."

"I can't marry you."

"Why?"

She gestured to her workroom, to her dye-stained shirt. "Look around you. Face it, Cameron. I'm not political wife material. I don't wear designer clothes or have manicured nails. I don't patronize the 'in' caterers or read the right books."

"Do you think I care about those things?"

She was stalling. And doing a poor job of it. Her lips quivered into a smile. A poor imitation of her usual one, granted. But a smile. She hung onto it for all she was worth. Right now, it was all she had.

"I'm asking you to marry me," he said. "Not chair a committee."

"Why not? Why not ask me to chair a committee?"

He made a rude noise. "Because you don't do that kind of thing. I won't ask you to be anything other than what you are."

She ignored the latter statement to focus on the first. "You're right, I don't do that kind of thing. Not because I can't. But because I choose not to." She took a deep breath and prayed for the strength to say what needed to be said. "Just like I choose not to marry you."

"You *choose?* What makes you think that you can *choose* to live without me, that you can *choose* to stop loving me?"

A sob hitched in her throat. How could he believe she could ever stop loving him? Maybe it was for the best. She hardened her voice. And her heart.

"What's the matter, Senator? Can't you take rejection?"

The flash in his eyes erupted into flames. "If you want to lie to me, go ahead. But don't do it to yourself." His voice quieted. "You can give me all the excuses you want to about why you can't marry me. But at least be honest with yourself. You're a coward. You're afraid to take a chance. Because of the past."

"Okay. I'm afraid. I can't lose you like I did my mother."

"You won't lose me."

"How do you know?"

He didn't. He focused on what he did know. "I love you. Tell me you love me."

That part was easy. Of course she loved him. How could she not? He was everything she ever wanted, everything she ever dreamed of, everything she ever needed.

Obediently, she said the words. "I love you."

"Now tell me you'll spend the rest of your life with me." Though his words were light, she sensed the pain beneath them. The fear.

She longed to wipe away that pain, to put an end to his fear. A few simple words from her and she could erase both. But there was nothing simple about them. Those same words would destroy her.

And if she had her way, if he became something other than what he was, what would that do to him?

It would destroy him as surely as the assassin's bullet she feared. It would also destroy their love. Not at first, perhaps. But eventually. His love would turn to hate. And that she could not endure.

"I can't."

"You mean you won't."

"I mean I can't."

Even through the pain and tears, she

wanted him, needed him, loved him.

The heat died from his eyes, and with it, the rest of his anger. He loved her. If she could only see past her fear, she'd know that nothing else mattered.

She was a maddening blend of toughness and vulnerability. A rueful smile turned up his lips as he imagined her reaction to that. She'd deny the latter with her last breath.

Eve believed herself to be strong. And she was. What she didn't realize was that strength didn't have to stand alone. If only she accepted that admitting need — in particular, needing someone else — didn't translate into weakness.

"She loved me." Her voice wobbled, but she didn't notice. Neither did she notice the first tear that spilled over and slipped down her cheek.

But Daniel did. He brushed at the tear, caught it on the blunt pad of his fingertip. It glistened against his tanned skin, a diamond born of pain.

"Don't," he begged. Tears — her tears — reduced him to begging. He was angry. Not at her. But at fate, which had set their paths in motion years before they'd ever met, at a madman who'd destroyed so much with his hatred, at what might have been if . . . if only . . .

"I understand your fears. Maybe only in a small way," he added when he saw that she was about to object. "We'll work through them. Together." He took her hand, felt the nerves there, the strain. "We'll deal with it."

He, better than most, knew the power of words. Words could persuade, convince, sell. Their influence was immeasurable. He'd used them all his life, first in private practice, then in the Senate. He'd never felt their inadequacy as he did now.

The pain in Eve's eyes hadn't lessened. If anything, it had intensified. He'd done that. And hated himself for it.

The tears came then, breaking through the dam of her self-imposed control.

Daniel took her into his arms and held on. He ached for her, wishing he could take the pain from her and make it his own. A fierce protectiveness swept over him along with an intense frustration that he was powerless to erase the past.

"I have loved you from the beginning," he said, unable to bear the silence any longer.

"And I will love you until the end." She kissed him, so sweetly, so fiercely that his hopes soared until he understood. She was telling him good-bye.

Chapter Nine

Eve didn't believe in halfway measures. Not in joy. Not in grief. She'd grieved for her mother. It had been the grief of a child, but no less real for that.

Her grief now was that of a woman. But inside she still felt like a little girl.

If she allowed herself, she could still remember, still hear the two plops that the gun with its silencer had made. Security police had thrown her to the ground, along with her father and everyone else standing nearby.

But it had been too late. Even at thirteen years old, she'd recognized death. Her mother, who had always seemed so alive, so vital, was dead. Eve had promised herself then and there that she'd never put herself in that position again.

No one had paid attention to the vows made by a child. Her father had grieved with her, wiped Eve's tears, told her that her mother was in heaven. But even he had failed to understand the depth of Eve's fear, the terror that still gripped her.

She took a breath — a steadying one — and reminded herself she was free of that. Free but for the memories. How did you ever rid yourself of memories?

There'd been the trial. She hadn't attended, of course. Hadn't been allowed to attend. But she'd read about it. Her father, her aunt, the houseful of servants, had tried to keep the papers from her.

In the end, she'd had her way. The truth, she'd told her father, was what her mother had fought for in life. In her death, her daughter could ask for no less.

Just the thought of tying her life to someone destined to enter the race for the most powerful office on earth was enough to bring back the old nightmares.

No, she couldn't — she wouldn't — do it. She felt as though she'd been dropped into a bottomless pit of despair with no means of escape. A grief so devastating that it brought her to her knees grabbed hold of her. She wrapped her arms around her knees and rocked back and forth. She didn't cry daintily as some women did, a few tears to glisten like pretty diamonds on the lashes. No, hers came in great gushing torrents, noisy, harsh sobs that shook her until she was as limp as a rag doll.

It was there that Carla found her. A call from Daniel that Eve might need her had her arranging for a baby-sitter and rushing to her friend's home.

Carla took in the situation in a glance. Heedless of the clay-smeared floor, she dropped to her knees and hugged her friend.

Great sobs racked Eve's body, but Carla held on. She didn't bother with words. Words didn't heal. Love healed; unfortunately, it could also hurt. In Eve's case, hurt didn't begin to describe it. The pain and despair in her eyes tore at Carla's heart, and she felt her own eyes sting with tears.

As the sobs eased, Eve sagged against Carla, spent and broken.

"I can't be . . . He wants me to . . . I love him, but I can't do it."

Carla didn't need any explanation to interpret the disjointed words. "Did Daniel ask you to marry him?"

"Weeks ago. I promised I'd give him my answer when we got back from Washington. I thought maybe . . . and then I remembered. Everything. I can't."

Two such small words shouldn't hold so

much pain. Carla remembered back to her own rocky courtship with Sam. There'd been a time when she doubted they could find a common ground, much less enough to build a lifetime upon, a time when she'd allowed her head to rule her heart. In the end, she'd realized her heart had been right all the time. But that couldn't be forced. Eve would have to come to that conclusion all by herself.

Eve sniffled one more time before determinedly wiping her eyes. "He'll refuse to run for office if I ask him to."

"But you won't." Carla didn't have to ask. She knew her friend well enough to know Eve would never ask Daniel to make a choice like that, to sacrifice what he was for what she wanted him to be.

"No. I won't." Eve grabbed her arms and hugged herself. "I might want to. But I won't."

"Love doesn't give easy choices, does it?"

Eve lips quivered into a smile. "No. It doesn't."

Carla took a deep breath. As much as she loved her Eve, *because* she loved her, she couldn't let Eve throw away a chance at happiness. "Daniel's a strong man. He won't take chances."

"Don't you think I know that? But I can't — I won't — risk it."

The words were torn from her friend, and Carla ached for what she had to do. "When are you going to stop running?"

"I'm not —"

"You've been running since you were thirteen years old."

Eve looked at her with accusing eyes. "I thought you were my friend."

"I am. That's why I can't let you keep running away."

"You think that's what I'm doing?"

"I know it is." The pain in Eve's eyes nearly undid Carla, but she forced herself to continue. "You're punishing Daniel for something that *might* happen."

"It's happened before. My mother . . ." The words ended in another whimper, and Carla reached for Eve.

"I know. I know."

They stayed there, on the cold floor, until Carla's muscles cramped. Struggling to her feet, she brought Eve up with her and settled her on the stool.

With the admonition to Eve to stay put, Carla headed to the kitchen. She went through the cupboards, looking for something high on sugar and low on nutrition. She settled for a box of chocolate chip cookies.

She slit open the box, arranged a dozen or so on a plate, poured two glasses of milk, and carried it all back to the work-room on a tray. She handed the plate of cookies to Eve, amused when her friend scooped out a handful.

Mindful of the ten extra pounds of baby weight she still had to lose, Carla took two instead of the half dozen she would have preferred. By unspoken agreement, conversation was temporarily halted as they munched away.

Eve sighed. "I needed that."

Carla gave the remaining cookies a regretful glance and finished her milk. "What are you going to do?" she asked.

Eve popped another cookie into her mouth. "Eating myself into oblivion sounds good." The laugh that followed sounded forced.

Carla knew her friend was trying to pull herself together and wished she knew how to help. She was a minister, for goodness sake. She'd counseled dozens of people, helping them put their lives back together. Why couldn't she do the same for Eve?

Carla hugged her again. "Call me tomorrow." She checked her watch. Zach was nursing every two hours, and she needed to get home.

Eve thanked her and promised she'd call even though she knew she wouldn't. She tumbled into bed that night. She didn't know why she'd thought she could sleep, but she went through the motions. She followed her normal nighttime routine, hoping . . . praying . . . that the late hour and her own exhaustion would catch up with her.

When sleep failed to come, she wasn't surprised. Life didn't work that way. How had she even dared hope she could blot out the pain with the oblivion of sleep? And how could she forget the accusations Daniel had flung at her?

He'd been right. She accepted that just as she accepted her own culpability. She was a coward. The word mocked her. When sleep finally claimed her, the word was still there, an indictment of her culpability, of what she'd given up.

Morning came, and with it, the rain. Dense clouds thickened the sky; humidity clogged the air. She normally enjoyed a rainy day. Rain cleansed. Today, though, the dreary colors mirrored her own mood, intensifying it until it threatened to consume her.

She wouldn't give into it, she vowed. She'd always despised people who indulged in pity parties. Enough was enough. She showered, dressed, and pretended that her heart wasn't breaking.

The gloomy weather didn't discourage customers. She was busy from the moment she opened the door for business. Grateful for the activity, she waited on people, chatting with them with a cheerfulness that she hoped didn't sound as forced as it felt.

Two women browsed among the piles of woven rugs, destroying the neat arrangement. Eve kept her patience, showing them one after another until they made up their minds. In the end, they bought two apiece, with a promise to return.

By the end of the day, she was weary beyond the belief. She fixed a salad for dinner and forced herself to eat it. The future stretched before her, a bleak expanse of empty days and emptier nights.

But there'd be safety. She clung to that. Somehow, though, it was cold comfort as she pictured a life without Daniel in it.

She loved him, but sometimes love wasn't enough. She silently railed against the fates that had thrown them together and then torn them apart. Love didn't see you through the pain of being left by yourself. She wouldn't risk it, couldn't risk it.

And what do you have now? a voice

taunted. Wasn't she equally alone, equally bereft through her own choice to push Daniel out of her life?

She turned to stare out the window, seeing not the ice-encrusted trees but her own reflection. The image didn't please her. Even the frost-dusted glass failed to disguise the pain in her eyes, a pain born of loneliness.

She had thought she'd known herself, was so sure that she knew what she wanted, what she needed. Now those certainties had been swept away, forever banished by memories of a man with serious eyes and lips that had a tendency to turn up at the corners when he thought no one was looking.

Being alone had never bothered her before. It was a choice she'd made consciously, accepting the consequences. But she was discovering choosing to be alone was a far cry from the emptiness that accompanied loneliness.

Wasn't that what she wanted? To be alone? To depend upon no one but herself? Her treacherous heart remembered how full it had begun to feel when Daniel had been in her life. That she had no one to blame but herself did nothing to relieve her misery.

Arms wrapped around her legs, she rested her head on her knees and wept for what might have been.

Night gave way to morning. The sun had chased away the last of yesterday's gloom. Shafts of buttery color shone through the sheer curtains, creating a patchwork quilt of light and darkness across the floor. In the sunbeams, dust motes danced and frolicked.

Eve concentrated on the ever-shifting pattern of light. If she concentrated hard enough, if she didn't give herself time to think, she could put Daniel out of her mind.

Liar.

A harsh voice mocked her efforts. *Liar,* it taunted again. Daniel was in her mind to stay. No trickery, no amount of will, no self-discipline could banish him.

And so she accepted that. Daniel was part of her life. She had no choice in the matter. What she did have choice in was how she dealt with it. She didn't intend on staying around to sulk in her misery.

Action was called for. Within a few minutes, she'd arranged with Ron to watch the store for the next few afternoons. Another few minutes saw her finishing packing a suitcase.

She'd never been a coward. It was one of her vanities. She'd faced life head-on, meeting it, embracing it, cherishing it because she knew how easily, how very easily, it could be ripped away.

Hadn't she gone bungee-jumping when a friend had suggested it? Never mind that she'd given it up after making several successful jumps because it failed to excite her after the initial thrill.

What about skydiving? And hang gliding? Didn't the fact that she'd tried them and more prove she wasn't afraid of anything?

Of course she wasn't a coward. Cowards shied away from life, hiding from it, cowering from risks, afraid to meet the challenges she ran to greet.

And what about starting her own business? No coward ever braved the miles of bureaucratic red tape involved in licensing, figuring out taxes, insurance forms, employee benefits, and the myriad of other details necessary to get a business off the ground.

Having convinced herself she was not — had never been — a coward, she left the shop.

It wasn't running away. She was simply taking a trip. A long overdue vacation.

Perfectly understandable.

Then why did it feel so much like running away?

On a muttered curse, Daniel yanked up the phone and punched out Eve's number. He'd given her two days. It was time they talked. His lips curved when he heard her voice, but the smile died the moment he realized it was a recording, informing him that she was unavailable.

He considered leaving a message, but hung up instead. What was he supposed to say? Don't send me away. I need you. I love you. I can't live without you.

Shaking his head, he paced the room. For the first time in his life, he didn't know what to do. He'd been so smug, so sure that he could convince her to forget her fears. The arrogance of it stunned him. How had he thought he could wipe away the fears of a lifetime?

He'd known Eve for a few short weeks. She'd lived with her nightmares for years. He knew she loved him. But it wasn't enough. The knowledge ripped into his heart. Angry thoughts of what might have been, what could have been, filled his head, his heart.

Not that he was giving up.

He had plenty to keep him busy. Even when Congress was in recess, the demands didn't stop. If anything, they picked up. He didn't have time to brood over one exasperating, infuriating, irritating woman, even if she was the woman he loved heart, body, and soul.

But that was exactly what he was doing.

Reports to draft, letters to answer, campaigning for reelection, all should have filled the days. And they did. But they failed to fill the emptiness of the nights. Nothing, not even the bone-deep exhaustion he worked himself into, could erase the long hours between night and morning.

When he tried Eve's number the following day, he got the answering machine again. More annoyed than worried, he figured he'd try again. The pattern repeated itself until he accepted the fact that she was gone.

Daniel didn't have time to brood. A meeting in Washington called by party leaders had him catching the red-eye to the nation's capital.

The kid gloves were off now. The top men and women in the party grilled him. Nothing was too trivial to escape their notice; nothing was too personal to address.

Daniel thought he was prepared. Nothing, though, could have prepared him for this kind of prying into his private life. When Eve's name came up, he tensed. He managed to answer the questions, but, as he'd instructed witnesses during his stint as a trial lawyer, he didn't volunteer any information.

Apparently, he passed the test, for the senior member of the group nodded. "You'll do."

Back in his office, Daniel received a call from Sam saying he was in town for a seminar. Agreeing to meet his friend at his health club, Daniel hoped to learn some news about Eve.

Daniel sliced with his racket, letting out a grunt as the ball slammed into the wall with a gratifying *whump*. He'd missed his weekly game because of his stay in Saratoga. He was glad to see he hadn't lost his touch.

Sam Hastings removed his protective goggles. "You trying to beat some kind of record or something? Or maybe you're just trying to forget a certain redhead."

Though Daniel was glad to see his friend, he could do without the inquisition.

"Nah. Just trying to beat you."

"You got some kind of backhand there." Sam ripped off his canary-yellow sweat-band and wiped his forehead. "What do you say we call it quits for today?"

"Fine by me." Daniel slumped against the wall. "You didn't look too shabby out there yourself."

"Pull the other one," his friend said, grimacing as he slid to the floor. "But thanks for the kind words. Ever since I coached a girls' basketball game and got the stuffing knocked out of me, Carla's been after me to get in some exercise."

The mention of Sam's wife was just the opening Daniel had been hoping for. "How are Carla and Zach?"

"Fine." Sam gave him a shrewd look. "It's only a guess, but I'd say it was Eve you're interested in. Am I right?"

As always, the mention of Eve's name tore at Daniel's heart. Since he'd returned to Washington, he'd had to struggle every day, every hour, every minute to keep her from his thoughts and to focus on his job. He'd failed miserably. "And if you were?"

"I'd wish you luck."

Daniel couldn't doubt the sincerity in his friend's voice.

"You in for the long haul, buddy?" Sam asked.

"Yeah." The word came without hesitation. "Yeah. I am."

"Congratulations. I never thought I'd see the day you took the plunge."

"I could say the same to you." The comment, which he'd intended to tease, came out sounding more like an accusation. Daniel flushed. He wished his friend nothing but happiness, but he'd sounded like a selfish jerk, begrudging Sam what he, Daniel, had failed to find for himself.

Sam didn't appear annoyed. If anything, he looked amused. "Yeah. There's nothing like it. Once you get your feet wet, you'll understand. Carla, and now Zach, are my life. If I didn't have them, I don't know what I'd do."

Daniel stared at his friend. He'd never known Sam to wax poetic before. He wanted to smile, but couldn't seem to make his lips obey.

The amusement faded from Sam's eyes. "If you love her, don't let her go."

"Do you think I wanted to?" Daniel demanded, the words ripped from him. "Do you think I wanted this? Any of this? A woman who has no need for me?"

"You don't believe that," Sam said quietly.

"No." Daniel shook his head. He didn't believe it. Any more than he believed he could change the past. He knew Eve loved him, needed him, just as he loved, needed her. What he didn't know was how to erase her fears.

"Is she back?" There, he'd said the words. Pride, be darned.

"Not yet. I'm sorry, Daniel." The sympathy in Sam's voice had Daniel tightening his lips. Now he was an object of pity.

The sympathetic words were knives to his soul. "Thanks for the game." He pushed himself up and headed to the showers.

Daniel couldn't concentrate. Even work had lost its challenge. No, that wasn't right, he decided. The challenge was still there. It was that his heart wasn't in it anymore.

He gave into the not-so-subtle demands of his staff and turned over work that should have gone to them to begin with. That soothed some of the ruffled feathers at work, but failed to ease the ache in his heart.

For as long as he could remember, work

had been a cure-all. No longer.

At his house, he loosened his tie and yanked it off, shedding his shirt as he headed to the bedroom. There, he shucked his pants and then rummaged through a drawer for a pair of comfortable sweats. Pulling them on, he decided to take a run. Maybe some exercise would clear the cobwebs from his mind. When he wasn't at the office, he tried to exorcise memories by pushing his body to the limit.

An hour later, the cobwebs remained. He knew he was only running from his problems. Unfortunately, no matter how much he pushed himself or how far he ran, he couldn't run away from his thoughts.

He returned home sweat-drenched and exhausted. Fifteen minutes in the shower solved the first problem, but didn't relieve the weariness that had dogged him since he'd returned from Saratoga.

His housekeeper's voice calling him to dinner prodded him to move faster. He finished dressing in jeans and a polo shirt. In the dining room, he noticed how ridiculous the one place setting appeared at the large glass-topped table. How had he failed to notice that until now? He picked at his food, ignoring Mrs. Carson's obvious displeasure.

"If you're not hungry, I'll clear the table," she said stiffly.

The reproach in her voice forced him to make an effort to appear to enjoy the meal. After five minutes of pushing the food around on his plate, he gave up. The cordon bleu meal failed to tempt his appetite. Nothing tempted his appetite these days.

His thoughts strayed to the pizza he'd shared with Eve. Stringy with cheese and hot with red pepper flakes, it had tasted like nectar. Other memories tumbled head over heels upon it.

Why did his mind pick now to remember the way her eyes lit up when she was happy? The gentleness of her voice as she comforted Zach? The sweetness of her smile when she looked at him? From there it was only a slight jump to think of the softness of her skin, the freckles that danced across her nose, the lushness of her lips.

He pushed his plate away and stood. All this because of a meal he couldn't bring himself to touch. Heaven only knew what would happen if he were to actually see her again.

The image took shape before the thought was fully formed. He needed to see her. Just the thought of her, and his heart shattered.

Anger, hot and urgent, filled him. Enough was enough. He'd given her time. Now it was his turn. He didn't intend to stop until he'd found her and convinced her that they belonged together. Somehow, he'd make her see what he'd known from the beginning — that they were meant for each other. Whatever it took, he'd make it happen.

If it meant giving up his Senate seat and a shot at the presidency, he'd do it. It was a small enough price to pay if it meant having Eve in his life.

Chapter Ten

The hurried trip to Saratoga had been for nothing. Eve still hadn't returned. After wandering aimlessly for hours, Daniel found himself at Sam and Carla's home. When he discovered Sam wasn't in, he was about to leave when Carla drew him inside.

He'd always liked the Hastings' home. It was the feeling of welcome he had whenever he entered it, the warmth that came from people who shared common beliefs and weren't afraid to act on them.

From Sam, he'd learned of Carla's commitment to helping the homeless. Daniel had frequently accompanied them to the shelters and used what he'd found there to draft a bill to fund inexpensive public housing.

Today, though, his thoughts weren't on shelters or bills before Congress.

"Eve's still not back," he said flatly.

What Carla saw in Daniel's face stirred

her compassion. She gestured to a chair. He slumped into it, the tired gesture saying more than words about his state of mind. She ached for him, for Eve, for the suffering they both endured.

Carla stood and crossed the room to where she kept the makings for tea. The herbal tea she chose was designed to soothe. Daniel Cameron looked in need of it. She handed him a mug and watched as he wrapped his fingers around it, as if he needed the warmth, though the room's temperature hovered near seventy.

He took a careful sip. "Do you know where she is?"

Regretfully, Carla shook her head. "I know she's hurting." She left the statement open.

He nodded. "I pushed her for a commitment."

Her silence was eloquent on what she felt about that. She hid a smile as Dan squirmed like a small boy sent to the principal's office.

"I acted like an idiot. I shouldn't have rushed her. It's just that . . . I love her so much." His voice hitched at the last, and her heart wept for him.

"Did she say anything before she left? Anything at all?" The question cost him, she could tell. Dan Cameron was a proud man, one unaccustomed to asking for anything. That he did so now was one more proof of the depth of his feelings for Eve.

"Just that she needed to get away for a while." Carla took his hand in hers. "It hurts, doesn't it?"

"Big time." He tried a smile. The compassion in her eyes confirmed what he already knew: his effort at a smile was a dismal failure.

Carla held out the only hope she could give him. "Eve said that she loved you."

The light in Daniel's eyes flared quickly before flickering out. "Not enough."

"How do you know?"

"If she loved me, she'd believe we could work things out."

"She's frightened."

"Don't you think I know that?" Carla looked startled at his outburst. "Sorry. I didn't mean —"

Carla sliced through his apology with a sharp gesture. "If you love her, give her the time she needs. Love sometimes means waiting."

She could see that Daniel didn't like hearing that. She tried another tack. "Did Sam ever tell you about how we got together?"

Daniel shook his head. "Only that the two of you met at a race and you whipped his . . . that you won."

A smile inched its way across her lips. "We managed to antagonize each other almost from the start. He thought I was some do-gooder and I thought he was just another politician." She smiled briefly. "Sorry."

He didn't appear offended by the reference. "But then you got together."

"Yeah. We got together, but we had our ups and downs. Things were good for a while. Then we let something come between us." The memory of the bitter words she and Sam had hurled at each other caused a shiver to skip down her spine. "It almost cost us everything."

"What got you back together?"

"We found that we were better together than we were apart."

"You know how I feel about her," he said.

The understanding in Carla's eyes convinced him she *did* understand.

All the frustration, all the hurt, all the anger poured out. "Telling her I loved her wasn't enough. Showing her wasn't enough. Nothing's enough. She doesn't know what she wants."

That wasn't true, he thought. She knew exactly what she wanted. And it wasn't him.

"I think you're underestimating Eve. And yourself."

"Am I?" he asked, unable to keep the bitterness from his voice.

Carla's nod was a ray of hope, and he found himself clinging to it.

"Eve's stronger than she thinks," she said. "She'll find her way back."

When the baby monitor picked up the sound of Zach crying in the nursery, Daniel surprised himself by offering to get the baby.

"He probably needs his diaper changed," Carla put in.

Daniel swallowed. "No problem."

"Mind if I tag along?"

Impatient squalls greeted them as they pushed open the door to the nursery.

Daniel was quick to realize that Zach had no use for him. He wanted his mother, and he wanted her now.

With a serene smile, Carla lifted the baby from his crib and set about the task of bathing him. She soothed him with nothing more than quiet murmurs and a promise he'd be getting his supper shortly. Zach stared back at her, seeming to understand every word.

Daniel could only look on in amazement as she finished the task of bathing, drying, and dressing the baby in a clean sleeper. Knowing that she probably wanted some privacy to feed him, Daniel excused himself and returned to the living room.

Some help he'd been, he thought with a self-deprecatory smile. He'd faced down opponents on the Senate floor, critics in the press, slander in the tabloids, and yet he'd been helpless in the face of the baby's distress.

When Carla, the now contented Zach in her arms, appeared within fifteen minutes, he stood.

"Would you like to hold him?" she asked.

Without waiting for his answer, she placed the precious bundle in Daniel's arms.

Automatically, Daniel snuggled Zach against him. The smell of just-washed baby drifted up to him, and he inhaled sharply. What would Eve think if she saw him now?

With a thimble-sized sigh, Zach settled against Daniel. The sigh turned to a yawn, the yawn to a sound suspiciously like a snore.

He liked the sweet weight of the sleeping child in his arms, the way the tiny head nestled in the crook of his elbow, the baby-soft breaths that escaped the rosebud-shaped mouth. There was a substantial feeling in holding the eight-pounds-plus baby, substantial as in truly mattering, substantial as in doing something important, substantial as in making a difference.

Isn't that what he claimed he wanted? To make a difference? Wasn't that why he'd chosen a career in public service? Could he achieve the same feeling of doing something substantial, of making a difference, in marrying and starting a family? He followed the train of thought to its natural conclusion. If he gave up his career, there'd be no obstacle standing between him and Eve.

He thought of the meeting he'd attended in Washington. A man didn't walk away from that kind of responsibility. But neither could he walk away from Eve.

He looked up to find Carla watching him, a knowing smile on her lips. "You feel it, don't you?"

He didn't need to ask what "it" was. He knew. The tender weight of a baby, the feel of barely begun life, the promise of beginnings. The *hope*. Yes, he felt it.

His nod was barely there, but he knew Carla had caught it.

Zach stirred. Instinctively, Daniel held him closer. “Shh. It’s all right.”

Carla motioned toward the nursery. “Time for his nap.” She lifted the baby into her arms.

Daniel tried not to imagine what he and Eve’s baby would look like. He tried not to feel bereft at the loss of the sleeping child in his arms. He tried not to feel at all.

But Eve’s face swam before his eyes, the sweet curve of her cheek, the fall of her hair, the tilt of her lips. He remembered each and every feature. Even more, he remembered her generous spirit, her zest for life, her joy in small things. And he ached for what he had lost.

When Carla returned, she went to him and touched his arm. “She’ll be back.”

“How do you know?”

“I know.”

He looked into her eyes and believed. Maybe because her words held the ring of truth. Maybe because he wanted to. Most probably because he *needed* to.

Later, Carla told Sam about Daniel’s visit.

“I’ve known Daniel for close to fifteen years.” Absently, Sam scratched George behind the ears. A deep rumble signaled the big dog’s pleasure. “He’s hurting.”

"So is Eve." Carla shifted Zach to her shoulder and patted his back. He rewarded her with a loud burp. "That's it, big boy. Get all those bubbles out of there."

Sam watched, his heart filling with love. Love. A small word. One that could bring unbelievable happiness. Or unbearable pain.

He could only pray that his friend would find what he had.

In her hotel room, Eve put out the pictures she always carried with her.

She stared at the one of her mother, its edges slightly bent, its colors muted. Her mother's face, so very like her own, stared back at her. Evelyn Dalton had been a strong woman, one who went after what she wanted with everything she had.

How had her daughter turned out to be such a coward?

The second picture was of her parents, taken at their last wedding anniversary. The love shining from their eyes hadn't dimmed with the years. It was there, bright and bold, for all who cared to look. Their smiles hadn't been for the camera, only for each other. Still, the camera had managed to capture the love that arched between them.

Unbidden, Daniel's voice, teasing and

tender, husky and hearty, echoed through her memory. The sound was so real, so powerful that she looked about, as if she'd conjured him up. All she had to do to start the memories coming was simply close her eyes and forget everything but the sound of him whispering her name.

But she was alone. Utterly, totally alone.

She set the picture aside and wandered to the window. Moonlight silvered the dark, quiet garden below. Shapes appeared, shifted, swayed in the breeze. A tug at the curtains had them opening, and the breeze cooled her heated skin. She inhaled deeply, needing the fresh air, as if it could banish the cobwebs from her mind.

Nothing could expel the memory of the anger in Daniel's eyes, though. That she deserved it only sharpened her pain, deepened her guilt.

But how could she have done anything different? She couldn't ask him to choose between her and what he was. She wouldn't love him as she did if he weren't the man he was.

The following morning, she threw her things into a suitcase. She hadn't known she was on her way to her father's home in Hershey, Pennsylvania, until she hit the interstate. When the realization came, she chuckled. Whenever she'd been upset as a little girl, she'd turned to her father. It seemed some things never changed.

She smiled as she pulled into the driveway and spotted him repairing the wrap-around porch of the century-old farmhouse. He'd bought the house five years ago after retiring from Georgetown University, where he'd taught law for thirty years. Slowly, he was renovating the house.

She parked the car and let herself out. "Daddy," she called, and ran to him.

He stuck a hammer in the carpenter's apron he wore and opened his arms. After hugging her, he scratched his head. "Did you tell me you were coming?"

The old joke raised the first genuine smile she'd felt in days. At sixty-nine, Willard Dalton still had the sharp mind that had kept law students on their toes for more than three decades, but he liked the image of the absentminded professor and often played it to the hilt.

Eve played along. "Of course I did. You just forgot."

After wrapping her in another hug, he opened the door and gestured her inside. "What brings you to see your old man?"

"Can't a girl want to see her favorite father?"

He stood her back and studied her. "What's going on with my Evie?"

He used the nickname rarely. That he did so now told her he knew she was hurting. The story poured out, and with it, a bucket of tears. When she'd dried her eyes, her father took her in his arms and rocked her, as he had when she'd been a child.

"You'd like him, Daddy," she whispered. "He's a good man. A decent, caring man who's going all the way to the top. He wants me to be with him."

"And you're afraid. Because of what happened to Evelyn."

She managed a nod.

"Your mother and I were some of the lucky ones."

She pulled back to stare at him, not sure she'd heard him correctly. "Lucky?"

"We had fifteen years together. Fifteen happy years. That's more than a lot of people have. Nothing is as dangerous as loving. Unless it's not loving at all."

She'd never heard her father talk like that before. Maybe she'd never listened.

"Your mother loved us," he said.

"Then why did she have to run for office? If she hadn't, she might still be . . ." She couldn't complete the sentence, couldn't say the word that hovered on her lips.

"Alive," her father finished the thought for her. "She wanted to make a difference. For you, for your children, for all the children. But she never forgot her most important role." A reminiscent smile touched his lips. "She used to say being a wife and mother was keeper of the present, mother of the future."

"Keeper of the present, mother of the future," she repeated. "Did she really mean that?"

"What do you think?"

Eve didn't have to wonder. She remembered the love that shimmered between her mother and her father, a love that the years hadn't dimmed. She also recalled the love her mother had lavished upon her. They hadn't had a lot of time together, but what they'd shared was a precious memory.

Something else her father had said snared her attention. "That's what Daniel says. He wants to make a difference."

"He sounds like a good man."

"He is," she said and knew it was the truth. Daniel *was* a good man. Perhaps a great one.

"You love him, don't you?" her father asked.

"With all my heart."

"Would it hurt any less if something

happened to him and you weren't married to him?"

Something happen to Daniel? The mere suggestion was unbearable, shortening her breath and lengthening her heartache.

"Would it?" he persisted.

Was the answer to all the other questions found in the answer to this one? Would the pain be any less if something happened to Daniel and they didn't belong to each other? Because they already did. Whether or not what they had was formalized with a marriage certificate, whether or not they legalized their feelings, whether they were together or apart, her heart already belonged to him.

She didn't need to think about it. "No." Whatever happened to Daniel happened to her.

"Then why not take whatever time you have? I wouldn't trade one of those years with your mother for all the safety, all the guarantees in the world. Not one."

Eve pressed her father's hand between her own. "I know how much you loved Mother."

His smile was a gentle rebuke. "No, you don't. Not yet. But you will. If you have enough courage to go to your young man and tell him what's in your heart."

Did she? Did she have enough courage? She wanted to believe she did. She wanted to believe it more than she'd ever wanted anything in her life.

"I love him."

"Then you know all that you need to."

"I do, don't I?"

The simplicity of the answer astounded her. Why hadn't she seen it before? She loved Daniel. And he loved her. At least, he had. Had she destroyed his love with her fear?

She hugged him. "Thanks, Daddy."

"Now that we've straightened out your life, stay and have dinner. Tomorrow is soon enough to start home."

The following morning, she was up before sunrise. "I'll call you," she said.

Her father held her close. "Give Daniel my best. And welcome him to the family."

"I will."

She drove with a reckless disregard for the speed limits, her carelessness fed by the pleadings of a desperate heart.

Pictures of the two of them together crowded her thoughts. Daniel with a cone of cotton candy in one hand and a footlong hot dog in the other. Daniel choosing a present for Carla. Daniel holding Zach in his arms. The steady gaze from his eyes, the smile that had a hint of seriousness beneath it.

A dozen other images, captured in such a short time, flitted through her mind, until they were whittled down to one: Daniel telling her that he loved her and asking her to marry him.

Please, she prayed silently. Please don't let it be too late.

She headed home. Home. It wasn't a matter of place, but one of the heart. And her heart belonged to Daniel.

He was everything she'd ever wanted. Love didn't come to order, she'd learned. Nor did it come with guarantees. The only certainty she had was that she wanted to spend the rest of her life with Daniel. Five years or fifty-five, she wanted every one of them with him.

She didn't have to look far. She found him in front of her shop, his head bowed as he leaned against the door. Her heart broke a little more as she understood that she'd done that.

She pulled into the driveway, not caring that the car angled onto the lawn. Yanking open the door, she climbed out. Daniel stared at her with an intensity, a longing she thought she'd never see again.

Did he move first, or did she? It didn't matter. Within moments, they were but a scant inch apart.

Each halted.

Each waited.

Each wondered what to say.

Daniel solved the problem by wrapping his arms around her waist, lifting her off her feet, and holding her to him as if he'd never let her go.

He crushed her to him, running his hands over her hair, her face, her shoulders, as if to reassure himself that she was, indeed, here. His lips found hers, hungry and eager, warm and tender.

When, at last, he put her from him, she started to tell him about her conversation with her father, what she'd learned about herself. "I —"

"No. I've got some things to say and you're going to listen."

"You don't under—"

"What I understand is that I love you and you love me." There. He'd said it. "I want to make memories with you. I want to grow old with you and have babies and grandbabies with red hair and golden eyes. I want you to teach them how to weave and for us to weave dreams together. I want the whole nine yards."

"So do I."

The words were delivered so softly that he barely caught them. "Say that again."

"So do I." More loudly. "So do I." Boldly now. "I love you." The words tumbled from her lips.

She caught her hand in his. "I took a look at all the scenarios. You could get killed by a madman's bullet." She put up her other hand to stop him when he would have protested. "I could prick my finger on my spinning wheel and sleep a hundred years." His lips were twitching now. "Or I might get mowed down by a bus. There are no guarantees. No absolutes. Except one."

"What's that?"

"This." She stood on tiptoe and pressed a kiss to his lips. "I love you. Whatever happens, that won't change. That won't ever change."

"I've been thinking. I could practice law. Or teach. I've always fancied myself a professor at some Ivy League school. I can see it now. I'd look very distinguished in jackets with leather patches on the elbows, have a cigar in the corner of my mouth, and lecture on very esoteric subjects."

The image filled him with revulsion, but

for Eve, he'd do it. He'd understood during the last weeks that he'd do anything, sacrifice anything, *be* anything, if it meant having her in his life.

For a moment, she pictured sharing an ordinary life with Daniel, one without the press and the potential dangers. One filled with station wagons, car pools, Saturday nights at the movies, and Sunday dinners with the family. Even as the picture took shape in her mind, she knew it wasn't right.

"Running for president . . . making a difference to this country, that's your dream, that's what you were meant to do. That's your destiny."

"That was before I knew you." He closed his hands over her shoulders, bringing her closer. "*You* are my dream. My destiny. You're everything I ever wanted. None of it matters if it means I lose you. If I do nothing but spend the rest of my life loving you, sharing with you, building a life with you, I'll have everything worth having, every dream worth dreaming, every wish worth wishing."

"You've forgotten one very important thing. I fell in love with *you,* not some hotshot lawyer or boring professor. You. Just the way you are." She took his hand in hers and pressed it to her lips. "Daniel, you're the most honorable man I know. How can I ask you to be any less? I won't promise to be a society leader or serve on committees. All I can promise is to love you."

"That's all I've ever wanted." He tugged her to him and held on tight. "*You're* all I ever wanted."

"You have me. For now. For always."

The employees of Thorndike Press hope you have enjoyed this Large Print book. All our Thorndike and Wheeler Large Print titles are designed for easy reading, and all our books are made to last. Other Thorndike Press Large Print books are available at your library, through selected bookstores, or directly from us.

For information about titles, please call:

(800) 223-1244

or visit our Web site at:

www.gale.com/thorndike
www.gale.com/wheeler

To share your comments, please write:

Publisher
Thorndike Press
295 Kennedy Memorial Drive
Waterville, ME 04901